# THE RISE OF THE WATER KINGDOM

Jamin Bradley

The Rise of the Water Kingdom
Published by Jamin Bradley

Print ISBN: 9781686681592
© 2019 JAMIN BRADLEY
All rights reserved.

Cover photo by Alice Alinari.
Author picture designed by Lee Occleshaw of Stone Dragon Workshop.

All rights reserved. You may use brief quotations from this resource in presentations, articles and books. Otherwise, no part of this book may be reproduced or transmitted in any form or by any means, electronic or mechanical, including photocopying and recording, or by any information storage and retrieval system, without permission in writing from the author.

Questions and comments can be sent directly to the author at: jaminbradley@me.com

# DEDICATION
## For Matt Shott

For the countless lengthy conversations we've had on sci-fi and fantasy over the years that have ensured that I kept an interest in the topic, eventually leading me to write a book in that direction.

# CONTENTS

| | | | |
|---|---|---|---|
| CHAPTER 1 | \::/ | Ghost Stories | 1 |
| CHAPTER 2 | \::/ | Fireflies | 7 |
| CHAPTER 3 | \::/ | New Names | 11 |
| CHAPTER 4 | \::/ | The Beach | 15 |
| CHAPTER 5 | \::/ | Conviction | 19 |
| CHAPTER 6 | \::/ | The Water Kingdom | 25 |
| CHAPTER 7 | \::/ | Old Friends | 37 |
| CHAPTER 8 | \::/ | Leaving Home | 53 |
| CHAPTER 9 | \::/ | Sea Monster | 57 |
| CHAPTER 10 | \::/ | The Shore | 65 |
| CHAPTER 11 | \::/ | The Family | 71 |
| CHAPTER 12 | \::/ | Son of Man | 77 |
| CHAPTER 13 | \::/ | Breakfast | 83 |
| CHAPTER 14 | \::/ | The Crowd | 89 |
| CHAPTER 15 | \::/ | Directions | 95 |
| CHAPTER 16 | \::/ | The Demonic Army | 103 |
| CHAPTER 17 | \::/ | Life and Death and After | 115 |
| CHAPTER 18 | \::/ | The Ascent | 123 |
| CHAPTER 19 | \::/ | The Dragon's Lair | 131 |
| CHAPTER 20 | \::/ | The Inn | 141 |

| CHAPTER 21 | \::/ | Nico | 145 |
| CHAPTER 22 | \::/ | Old Salem | 149 |
| CHAPTER 23 | \::/ | A Holiday Feast | 153 |
| CHAPTER 24 | \::/ | The Garden | 161 |
| CHAPTER 25 | \::/ | The Religious Leaders | 167 |
| CHAPTER 26 | \::/ | Execution | 171 |
| CHAPTER 27 | \::/ | Chains | 177 |
| CHAPTER 28 | \::/ | The Keys | 181 |
| CHAPTER 29 | \::/ | Rain | 183 |
| WRITER'S NOTE | \::/ | Allegory | 187 |
| ABOUT THE AUTHOR | \::/ | Jamin Bradley | 189 |

# CHAPTER 1
## GHOST STORIES

Brennan sat on a decaying log deep in the woods, close to the dying flames of a campfire he had started sometime ago. His sister, Kahli, laid fast asleep on the other side of the embers with a heavy knit blanket covering everything but her dark hair. With his head in one hand, he used his other to stroke the ashes with a long stick he had been using to keep the fire going all night. His eyes were heavy with sleep and he had been shaking his head sporadically to keep himself awake from the lullabies of crickets and the hypnotizing glow of fireflies. He would have given into their song by now had it not been for his anxiety.

It wasn't the open air that made him nervous–the woods had proven safe enough over the past two days–but Kahli's cough had grown more vicious and desperate by the day. At this point it seemed like a long shot that they'd get to the hospital before the unknown disease had completely taken over.

# GHOST STORIES

Brennan had noticed the signs far too late, it seemed. It started with migraines and evolved into long naps followed by a sore throat. The first two conditions seemed nothing to worry about, but now all Brennan could do was worry. Not only should he have sought help sooner, but he had next to no money to care for the bill he would certainly inherit.

The sound of Kahli viciously coughing in her sleep stopped Brennan from drifting off. He stood up quickly to spur himself awake as well as to protect himself. He could have sworn he had seen–or felt–a shadowy figure hovering over his shoulder. His heart raced as he walked around the campfire and picked up twigs and branches to throw into the dying flames.

*You really need to sleep,* Brennan told himself. *You're going to get Kahli killed if you don't. Maybe you would have reached the hospital by now if you had slept better the last few days. Her death is going to be on your hands if you don't get it together. Then how will you live with yourself? You already waited too long to take her in for help, you idiot. And why? Because you were afraid to spend money?* Brennan knit his brow angrily at himself. "You're so stupid," he whispered.

*You don't deserve to live,* said the shadow over his shoulder.

"And you don't deserve to live," Brennan said to himself.

*The world would be better without you anyways,* the shadow's voice reverberated through his mind.

"The world would be better without me," Brennan whispered angrily.

*Perhaps the most humane thing you can do is to kill her quietly and then yourself,* said the shadow.

Brennan paused. His lips both stung and felt numb at the same time. What had he been saying?

*Say it,* said the shadow.

"I..." stuttered Brennan. "What?"

Suddenly, Brennan realized he was staring right into a dark and shadowy hallucination of himself that had deep caverns for eyes. It had a tail that seemed to stretch from Kahli's stomach. Brennan's heart pounded.

"Perhaps," stated a smooth deep voice. "Perhaps the most *loving* thing you can do for her is to end her sickness while she's sleeping and then end your own pain." The spirit tilted its head to the left understandingly and smiled with the right side of its mouth. "Of course you would never *want* to do such a thing–that's completely understandable. But tough situations often require tough decisions," it continued.

The bags under Brennan's eyes spoke of his desperation. This was madness, was it not? A hallucination of sorts playing upon the strings of a dark part of his psyche. He would never do such a thing! ... Would he?

The hazy vision of himself morphed into an innocent portrayal of Kahli that had a deep look of sadness underneath her cavern eyes. "Do it for me," it spoke. *Like you did for Mom,* raced a voice through his mind.

He, of course, hadn't taken his mother's life. She had lost it trying to save him from falling through the ice one winter. It was hardly his fault. The winter had been so heavy that year that no one could tell the difference between solid ground and a frozen lake. In fact, she had led him onto the lake, unaware that she had done so until she heard the thunderous crack of the ice breaking. In that moment she made the quick decision to push Brennan backwards and then fell through, never to be seen again.

# GHOST STORIES

The memory played out in Brennan's mind more vividly than ever before as tears began to flow from his eyes. He knew that what had happened wasn't his fault–everyone in town had reiterated that to him–but his soul had never fully agreed with him. And now all of that confusion and inner-turmoil had been drawn up before him and acknowledged by this... this thing.

"Do it for me like you did for Mom," said the dark vision of Kahli.

"Now wait just a second," said Brennan. "I didn't do anything to Mom!"

"Oh?" questioned the shadow. "Hadn't that winter left her with a pretty severe cough herself?"

Brennan flinched. "Well, sure, but that wasn't the same!"

"It wasn't?" asked the ghost. "Are you sure you didn't subconsciously lead her onto the ice to end her sickness? Didn't you notice you were on the ice? Where were all the trees?"

A confused look came over Brennan's face. "I mean, I suppose it's possible I wondered about that, but I was a young child at the time! I can hardly be blamed for–"

A cold wind blew out what was left of the fire as the spirit vanished and the crickets stopped chirping. Even the fireflies stopped glowing. It was pitch black and the whole forest was unnaturally still.

"Kahli!" exclaimed Brennan as he stumbled through the darkness for her body. He tripped over her feet and fell to the ground. He then squirmed up to her and held her tightly to protect her. He couldn't see her face, but he could feel a fever radiating from her forehead.

"Brennan," said an imitation of his mother's voice that echoed through every corner of the forest. He knew it was an imitation because there was something sickly about it. It had her tone, but not her character. "Thank you for leading me onto the ice. I was very sick at the time and you stopped me from having to endure what Kahli is going through now."

Brennan began to cry as he held Kahli even tighter.

"Please," said the imitation. "Do what you need to do. Do what you did for me."

There was silence for a moment… And then Brennan's voice pierced through the darkness. "No!" he yelled. "I will never do what you say! And what you say never happened!"

The campfire suddenly lit up like a bonfire and burned Brennan's forearms. It was so hot that he instantly let go of his sister and rolled away. He then stood up to pull her away from the flames, but she began to stand up on her own.

"Then I will take your life before I submit myself to the flames!" she declared, her eyes completely black.

Brennan was surprisingly coherent of the situation at this point. While he knew this was indeed his sister's body in front of him, he knew the voice was not hers. Her words carried the same problem as his mother's a moment ago —right tone, wrong character.

She grabbed him by the arms with an unnatural strength and tossed him towards the bonfire.

The spirit snickered. "Would you like to do the honors, or should I?" It said as it pinned him to the ground and started to push his right hand toward the flame. Brennan cried out as the heat seared his flesh a little bit more with every inch.

"Kahli!" he yelled. "Kahli, I know you're in there! Come back to me!"

"Kahli is gone," hissed the spirit. "Or will be soon," it smirked.

Brennan screamed as his fingers began to enter the flame and blister, when suddenly, the bonfire dissipated to embers.

# CHAPTER 2
## Fireflies

Suddenly the spirit stepped back. "What is that unbearable noise?" it hissed.

The forest went quiet once again as Brennan's ears perked up, searching for the same sound the spirit was hearing. He heard the faint sound of something, but his fingers hurt too much to concentrate.

Kahli fell to her knees and put her hands over her ears while her eyes searched rapidly in every direction. "That's enough!" barked the spirit. "No more! Please, I beg you! Stop the torment!"

Brennan could hear the noise a little more clearly now. It sounded like a man was humming in the distance. It was a beautiful little melody–an ear worm bound to get stuck in anyone's head. In fact, it was so beautiful that the pain in Brennan's hand began to fade to the point that he forgot it was even there.

# FIREFLIES

The fireflies began to flash to the tune, almost as though they were sheet music—their bioluminescence in sync with the pitch and length of each note hummed.

"Stop it!" screeched the spirit.

But the noise didn't stop. Instead, it grew louder and louder, as did the crickets. In fact, Brennan could have sworn they were chirping in harmony to the song. The noise crescendoed as the fireflies joined in with an unblinking, steady light.

Brennan slowly rose to his feet and looked at the bugs in wonder. He imagined that this was what it must look like to stand in the middle of space and look at the stars. Even though it was the middle of the night, he could see for miles in every direction. And he could also now see the man humming the tune as he approached them.

Tears fell from Kahli's cheeks. "Why?" the spirit asked as she fell on her side with her hands over her ears. "You've come too soon! We still had more time!"

The man knelt down next to Kahli and looked into her tear-soaked eyes as Brennan watched from a few feet away. He could see a change in her expression—a look in her eyes that seemed more herself than the evil spirit's.

The man put his hand on the girl's cheek and looked deep into her soul. "Hello," he said with a peaceful smile that changed the heavy atmosphere around him. "I was shown a glimpse of you here this morning, so I have come to meet you."

Kahli raised herself onto her knees and then looked into the man's eyes. She opened her mouth to say something, but then her eyes turned dark and she hissed. The man didn't flinch, though his demeanor did turn serious. He just looked deeper into Kahli's eyes and then said, "Go."

Instantly a shadowy residue evaporated out of Kahli's back and dissipated into the air, causing the whole forest to suddenly feel a bit lighter and freer. Brennan could have sworn that in the midst of it all he saw a bright light shoot out of the man's chest and expel the spirit from Kahli, but it happened so quickly that he wasn't sure if it was just the fireflies or a flicker from the campfire.

"Stand up, dear one," said the man as his face returned to a smile. Kahli looked cautiously into his eyes. "It's okay. I know you're tired, but have faith and find new strength."

Brennan's eyes were wide open as the stranger took Kahli's hand and pulled her to her feet. She looked like a completely different person. Her skin no longer looked sickly, her eyes no longer tired, and her facial expression finally looked like her own. She cleared her throat to test the soreness and found none.

Though she was full of strength, she immediately collapsed into the man's chest and cried tears of overwhelming joy. The man held her compassionately as Brennan stood at a distance, unsure of what to say.

"You're looking a bit better, too," said the man as he pointed towards Brennan's hand. Brennan held it up in the bright light of the fireflies. There were no blisters—no sign that there had ever been any physical harm done to him.

# CHAPTER 3
## New Names

"Who are you?" asked Brennan. And then catching a subtle glow coming from the man's body, he asked, "*What* are you?"

The man laughed as he patted Kahli softly on the back. "Whatever do you mean, *what* am I?"

"I mean, there's like… an unnatural glow about you," answered Brennan. "Not to mention the whole thing with the fireflies and the crickets and that… demon?"

"You see a glow, do you?" the man smirked.

Brennan tilted his head and raised an eyebrow in attempts to deduce if the glow was reality or the onset of sleep deprivation. It had been a strange night and reality wasn't really working the way he had always known it to.

"Uh," he winced. "Do you not see it?"

"Sometimes," he smiled. "It's typically not visible to the human eye. If you're seeing it then it's only because the Creator himself is allowing you to."

# NEW NAMES

"The Creator?" asked Brennan.

"Indeed," said the man as he released Kahli and walked towards Brennan. He took Brennan's hand and surveyed the healing. "And you know what that means."

"I do?" asked Brennan in confusion and amusement.

"It means you and I are connected now," the man said, staring intently at Brennan's fingers. "Does it hurt?" he asked.

"Uh, no. Not at all," Brennan replied.

"Good!" said the man as he slapped his right hand into Brennan's and shook it. "The name's Sarx."

"Brennan," he replied slowly. "And this is my sister, Kahli."

"Yes, yes, I know your names," said Sarx. "I was told them earlier."

"Told them?" Kahli asked with intrigue in her voice.

"Surely not the weirdest thing that's happened tonight," returned Brennan.

Sarx let out a heavy laugh. "Fair enough!" Brennan couldn't help but smile that his joke had been well received. "But yes, I was told your names ahead of time. And not only that, but I was also told your new names!"

*A complete stranger wants to rename us?* thought Brennan. *Okay, maybe that's the weirdest thing that's happened tonight.*

"I mean, I wouldn't consider it the weirdest thing," Sarx said with a grin, as though he had heard Brennan's very thought. "From the Creator's perspective, weird is anything outside of his will. So if he would like to bestow upon you a new name—well, nothing could be more normal, really."

"Look sir," started Brennan, "I perceive you are a wizard, but—"

"A wizard you say?" Sarx cut him short. "A wizard? I thought you said you saw the glow?"

"Yes—a spell of wizardry if ever there was one!" said Brennan.

Sarx laughed. "How can your eyes be opened to reality and yet your perception be so faulty?"

"I'm sorry!" Brennan said, throwing his hands in the air. "I don't have a lot of boxes to organize tonight's events in!"

"Then allow me to give you a few to help you out," said Sarx. "I am not a wizard that I should perform wizardry or a magician that I should do magic. I did not appeal to demons or ghosts or spirits or fairies to free your sister from those that made her their home."

"But I felt like I saw magic," said Brennan. "Something like a light that came out of you when you cast it out."

"You mean the Spirit of Light?" said Sarx as he began to glow once again.

"I guess," shrugged Brennan.

"That's very different from magic," said Sarx. "He is the Spirit of the one and only God—*the Creator*—and he guides and empowers me. He shows me what the Creator is doing and I act it out for others."

## NEW NAMES

"I see it too now!" Kahli exclaimed. "I see the light too!" Sarx had become so bright that Brennan had to shield his eyes with his hand. Soon the glow diminished and Brennan was able to see Sarx giving off a quiet chuckle.

"Alright you two, it's time to go," Sarx said. "But before we do you must receive your new names. Brennan, you will now be known as Mason. And Kahli, you will be called Junia."

The Spirit of Light bolted from Sarx and knocked them to the ground, flooding the siblings with warmth and love.

# CHAPTER 4
## THE BEACH

The siblings arose with the sun as different people. Rays of light beamed brightly across the ocean sky and warmed the sand below them.

"What on earth?" Mason mumbled under his breath as he slowly sat up and tried to get his bearings. He rubbed the sleep from the center of his eyes with his thumb and pointer finger and wiped the sand off his cheek. Then, in a moment of panic, he realized that he didn't see his sister anywhere and he leapt to his feet to find her. He looked left, then right, and then towards the ocean. He felt his blood coursing through his temple.

"Kahli!" he screamed at the top of his lungs, his voice breaking.

"What?" she asked as she slowly arose from her slumber, clutching her forehead as though his scream had given her an instant headache.

# THE BEACH

The pressure immediately dropped in his temple as he turned behind him to see his sister safe and sound. He dropped to his knees and put his hands on her cheeks. "Are you okay?" he asked.

"I'm fine," Junia replied. "More than fine, I think. Actually, I don't think I've ever felt quite this good."

Mason gazed into her eyes and saw a certain kind of peace in them that began to calm his nerves. As he settled down he began to realize that he, too, felt the same way. He couldn't help but admit that something was different. There was a certain beauty hovering about him or in him. It was as though beauty was a living entity that he could possess–*or was it that beauty possessed him?* It wasn't a beauty that was acknowledgeable by sight necessarily, but rather, something that one might recognize on a spiritual level–like a supernatural beauty of sorts. Mason could see it in his sister's eyes and feel it all over his own body.

"Look at you guys!" said Sarx as he gestured with open arms. "You aren't what you were! I can see it in your eyes."

"I don't quite understand it, but I know that's true," smiled Junia. "I can feel it in my bones–or deeper than that–like my very marrow is infected."

"Oh, I don't know that infection is the right word," smiled Sarx. "If anything, it's the opposite. You are–*at least for the time being*–as fully human as you can be. You are new creations with new names and new purpose."

Mason recounted the events of the night before. "Mason," he said aloud. "You said my name was Mason."

"And Junia," his sister chimed in.

"Indeed," replied Sarx.

"But why?" she asked.

"Why, what?" asked Sarx.

"Why the new names?" she elaborated.

Sarx grinned. "Well, names typically imply purpose, so I would imagine it has to do with that. If you don't understand them now, then the Spirit of Light will make their meaning clear in time."

Suddenly, a wave washed just far enough ashore to wet the bottom of their feet. Their heels sunk slightly into the newly wet sand as the wave pulled back into the ocean. There was something about the water that seemed pleasing to them. Even the icy ocean temperatures left something to be desired.

Sarx caught the glimmer in Mason's eye. "The sea grows hungry for you," he said. "For both of you."

Mason continued staring at his feet. "The water is insatiable," he admitted.

"Very much so," Junia added.

The cold wave made Mason's foot feel like it was burning—like how one's skin feels after being out in the snow too long—but despite the pain, for some reason he longed to be submerged in the water. The siblings slowly walked closer to the shore, as though in a trance.

"Freedom is beckoning you from under the ocean, but it comes at a great price," said Sarx from the distance.

"Anything would be worth it," said Junia as she stared at the waves. Mason nodded in agreement.

# THE BEACH

Suddenly, Sarx was right behind them, speaking into their ears. "Then you must pay with your lives," he said.

Both Mason and Junia broke out of the trance and turned around in surprise to see Sarx so close. Even more shocking was the fact that the beach was nowhere to be found. All they could see was the icy cold waters of freedom in every direction—including underneath them! They gasped at the sight of their feet standing on the waves in the middle of the ocean, but they had no time to react; for Sarx put three fingers on both of their foreheads and pushed them backwards into the water.

The two fell over in slow-motion as the back of their heads met the waves. They could see every droplet of water splash around them from the force of their bodies colliding with the waves. They listened as the treble of the current was blotted out by the bass of the ocean as their ears were slowly submerged.

Both of the siblings could tell the moment they hit the water that they would not be bouncing back up. They had no buoyancy. And as the last parts of their bodies were submerged into the icy cold waters, they made their peace with the air and embraced freedom—the kind that required the price of a life—a premise that struck Mason as a strange, and yet, desirable kind of slavery.

# CHAPTER 5
## Conviction

Mason and Junia gasped at the same time, unable to hold their breath any longer. Large bubbles floated out of their mouths and rose towards the blurry sun as their lungs filled with water. They were dead now–they knew it.

Yet at the same time they were alive. They had thought their final gasp would leave them fading into the darkness, but instead the ocean began to light up around them as they continued to fall deeper and deeper. The water that they thought would kill them instead became their fuel–as though they had become a different kind of creature. True, they still had bodies made of skin and felt in many regards very much the same, but at the same time they knew something had truly changed.

Perhaps they had just never seen themselves so clean before. It was as though every last speck of dirt and grime was being washed off of them in the frigid waters. They could see it coming off their skin and rising towards the surface.

## CONVICTION

Mason was surprised to see so much dirt leave his hands—by all means, he had always thought that dirt had been his very skin. But it was obvious now that it had been dirt all along—stubborn and caked onto every inch of his body. It was as though he was being made new.

Tears bubbled out of Junia's eyes as the dirt was washed off her arms. She had never been comfortable in her own skin. Something had always felt off about her body—as though she could be more beautiful if she spent more time doing herself up. Of course, even when she did do herself up she never believed anyone's compliments. "You look beautiful tonight," they'd say. "No I don't," she'd reply quickly, convinced that everyone was a liar. But now, for the first time, she believed. She was beautiful—*gorgeous even*.

As the dirt lifted off of her skin she felt like she could see it form into words—*ugly; gross; short; underwhelming*—and as each word floated away, she felt more and more secure in herself. The words tried to latch back onto her, but they couldn't seem to get a hold on her.

*Junia,* a voice breathed inside her head as an incredible warmth overtook her freezing bones. *You have always been beautiful.* Junia's eyes sprung wide open as she inhaled a deep breath of the intoxicating water. *Turn to me and I will make you even more beautiful.*

To the naked eye she didn't necessarily appear any different, but she knew the voice spoke truth. Something had been triggered in her that felt nearly impossible to undo. A truth had been spoken that was too big to be covered by a lie.

Then the waters grew colder and she was suddenly overcome with incredible conviction. Memories began to come to Kahli's mind—memories so vivid that they seemed to play out in the water around her. She turned to her left and saw a video of herself throwing up into some weeds—a habit she had been practicing for some time in efforts to become what she once considered beautiful. She then turned right and saw herself staring at her friends with a deep envy—perhaps, even a hatred. She believed that they had what she needed and that if she could just get a little bit of it for herself, she'd be better off.

In front of her she saw an image of a beautiful grown woman that looked like everything she aspired to be, sitting on a beach dock with an attractive man next to her. She knew that just yesterday, such a future would have been a dream come true.

But here underwater, even her eyes felt as though they had been made new, and all these images had a displeasure in them that she hadn't seen before. While the taste of vomit had never been enjoyable, she had always felt a strange measure of success after having thrown up. But in the vision she saw an unnaturally scrawny girl who looked more sickly than attractive and it filled her with remorse rather than accomplishment. On top of that, the girls she had always envied suddenly looked faker than they ever had. Their once beautiful makeup now made them look like clowns and their clothes were so tight that you couldn't help but laugh.

And though the grown version of herself wore a big smile, she knew it was all for show. As she continued to stare at the vision, it began to play in reverse, revealing that the lake below her beach dock was made out of her own tears. Teardrops ascended out of the lake and into her eyes until it had all dried up. Her future had been built on her grief.

The weight of a thousand sins suddenly felt as though they were latched onto her shoulders and she could recollect each one, all at the same time. She closed her eyes tightly as large tears continued to bubble out of her. The conviction was deep, but it was also necessary—firm, but also gentle. She took a deep breath and then whispered the only thing she could think to say: "I'm sorry."

And that was that. The weight was instantly gone. The sins unlatched. The final pieces of dirt evaporated. The dirt that was left on her took off at incredible speeds to the right and the left, destined to never meet again.

Brennan underwent his own experience—the same premise, but different sins. The things he had done to try to fit in with the other boys in town were played out in front of him in detail.

To his left he saw a memory of the time a friend dared him to steal a jewel out of a widow's home. He passed the test with flying colors. To his right he saw an old friend pressure him to drink until he could drink no more. After he had little sense left in him, another friend dared him to kiss a girl that was very much in love with him, but that he had no desire for at all. Again, he succumbed to the request.

The visions were incriminating. He was found out—a fraud. Everything he did, he did to impress. And everything he did now looked so wrong. Before this moment, he had thought of these memories as practical jokes—harmless dares to prove his worth. But now he saw them from a different perspective. A bright light began to shine on the memories as they rewound and started over. Brennan's heart broke at the pain of having to watch them all over again, especially because there were now changes made to the memories that made them much harder to stomach.

First, he saw the widow he had robbed. As her husband laid on his deathbed, about to breathe his last, he reached into his chest, pulled out his heart and handed it to his wife. With many tears she took the heart and placed it on her nightstand—the very place Brennan had stolen her jewelry from. You can only imagine Brennan's horror when he then watched himself enter the room and steal the man's heart. And the scene didn't change after he ran out the door with the heart. Instead, Brennan watched the woman wake up with the sheer terror of having been robbed of her greatest treasure. The conviction was so great that Brennan screamed.

And while he had been too drunk to remember the other memory very well, he now watched it in embarrassing detail. He saw himself as a beast. In a drunken stupor he bullied people and threatened to beat them up. He threw himself at girls and told them inappropriate jokes and made crude suggestions. And when they tried to brush him off, he called them names he didn't even know were in his vocabulary.

And then he had to watch the memory of the girl he kissed through her own eyes while feeling all the feelings she felt. She had had a crush on him since they were very young and she never thought he would return the sentiment. Yet there he was, about to give her her first kiss. Brennan was then ejected from her body, just in time to watch the beastly version of himself scratch her across the face and walk away laughing. The girl was so distraught that she pulled her heart out and left it on the ground.

*Mason,* said a voice in his head. *You do not need to impress me to earn my love. Turn to me and I will accept you.*

Mason's heart broke as some of the dirt that had left his body formed a hand and grabbed his ankle. It then began to pull his body back towards the surface. He felt so much shame. He had committed so many sins in attempts to be accepted and now the graphic nature of his crimes had been played out right before him. He was a monster, ravaging the people around him.

"I," he choked. "I am so... very... sorry."

*And you are so very forgiven,* said the voice as dirt flew off him in every direction.

As the apology left his mouth, the hand that was once pulling him upwards disintegrated and he began to descend further and further down into the ocean, quickly catching up with Junia and soon surpassing her. It had been evident that the weight released from him was heavier than hers had been.

And perhaps in this strange place, that had somehow given him the ability to sink quicker.

Mason's body eventually touched the ground, sending out a cloud of sand around him. Junia was not far behind.

# CHAPTER 6
## THE WATER KINGDOM

"Follow me," said Sarx as he reached down to pull the two up, his voice cutting through the water as though it were air itself. "The path here has been hard on you for sure, but now we're here."

As the two stood up, they beheld the most glorious kingdom before them. It stretched for miles and seemed to be the shape of a perfect cube. The siblings were mesmerized by its beauty as it was built out of the finest gems they had ever seen.

In front of them were beings that were hard to describe. They glowed so bright that it was difficult to make out any of their features. They were doing construction on the kingdom walls and seemed to be installing new gates on the building that stretched high, but were quite narrow.

The siblings approached the gates with Sarx in awe and fear; for a being of great size guarded the door. "Where exactly are we?" asked Mason, his voice trembling.

"You sound nervous," replied Sarx. "What's wrong?"

"I'm guessing he's afraid of that... that... large person at the door," answered Junia. "He looks like he means business."

"This is the kingdom of light, daughter," said Sarx. "Only love is practiced here—a quality of which you two are now made of and covered in. You have no need to fear your home."

"Our home?" the two asked in unison as they approached the gates, their bodies shaking in fear.

"Good afternoon angels!" Sarx greeted the construction workers.

"King Sarx!" exclaimed the large being as it knelt before him. "It is good to have you home, master."

"It is good to be home, Miguel!" laughed Sarx. "And how are your gate-keeping duties treating you today?"

Mason and Junia looked at each other with a wide-eyed expression as a new fear beset them. This awesome being was now kneeling before someone they had clearly not shown enough reverence for. *King Sarx?* they thought. *We're following the king of this place?* Then they began to think back over all the things they had recently said in hopes that they hadn't offended him in any way.

Their thoughts were interrupted by Miguel's thundering voice calling out, "All glory and honor and power to King Sarx!"

All the other angels stopped working on the gates and returned the battle cry. "All glory and honor and power to King Sarx!"

"Master Sarx!" one of the angels called out from the rafters. "Is the gate to your liking?"

"It looks great Gabe!" Sarx returned. "I can't wait to see what it looks like once you're done!"

The angel laughed, his glow shimmering in rhythm. "Forgive me master, but I still don't understand the point of the gates. Once the kingdom is installed, you mentioned you wanted them to remain open indefinitely. I'm not sure I understand their point?"

"Does a house require pictures on its walls to stand firm?" Sarx grinned.

"I suppose not," Gabe answered.

"Yet you still hang them to add meaning to a home," smiled Sarx.

"Good point!" the angel laughed. "You hear that boys? Doesn't matter if we're not using the doors—don't skimp on the labor!"

"Why would I skimp? I love this job!" exclaimed another angel. "Plus, I've already drawn up a few hundred decorative designs to choose from."

"Can't wait to see them Uri!" Sarx said as he turned around to find the siblings still staring intently at Miguel. "Again, you have no reason to fear. He's just here to secure the border for love's sake. Show him your papers."

"Our papers?" asked Junia.

"Yes," replied Sarx. "In your pockets."

The two reached into their pockets and pulled out a folded piece of paper that remained unaffected by the water. They unfolded it and read.

*By the decree of King Sarx, the person before you has been accepted beyond the great gates and is a citizen of the Kingdom of Heaven.* In the lower bottom corner was Sarx's signature in red ink. Or at least, they thought it was ink.

The two lifted their papers to the angel who then read them and smiled. "Welcome friends," he said with a thunderous voice. "May you enjoy your stay in the kingdom. Allow King Sarx to show you around. He is the best guide you could have." The two stuttered out a thank you and tripped over each other as they entered the gate.

"You have no need to be afraid of Miguel," said Sarx. He held out his hand as seven small lights, brighter than Miguel appeared. They seemed to be tiny, yet powerful angels. Mason and Junia covered their eyes for fear that they would go blind, yet they couldn't help looking at the light through their fingers. "All of the ranks of the kingdom are at my command," he said as the lights vanished into his fist.

As they walked through the gate, they found themselves stepping through a wall of water into open air–*that is, if you could call whatever this was, air*. It was almost as though the air itself was singing, or at least that was what it felt like to breathe it in–every melody softly quivering down their throats with the sweetest vibrato. And what water was left in this place was almost like crystal, flowing down a river that seemed to stretch through the entire cube.

As they walked down the golden streets that paved the city, the two were flooded with all kinds of feelings: Love, joy, and peace were at the center of it, with a hefty dash of fear that felt more appropriate than not. The two looked around in amazement. The whole city glowed like the sun and was painted with a rainbow of colors from the gems it was constructed with.

But perhaps the greatest thing they experienced was something that seemed near impossible to describe. It was as though the love, joy and peace they were feeling weren't actually their emotions, but rather an entity. It was as though it soaked every fiber of their being to the point that they were more drenched here in the open air of the kingdom than they were outside in the ocean. Every molecule of their body took it in and the two couldn't help but feel that every piece of them was trying to respond to the greatness of that love. As odd as it sounds, it even felt like their skin cells were trying to bow down.

"What's happening right now?" Mason inquired.

"What's that?" asked Sarx.

"I don't know, just… everything," said Mason, his eyes lit up with wonder.

"Ah," said Sarx. "You're not yet used to the feeling of uninhibited sacred space yet, are you?"

"This is sacred space?" asked Junia. "The entire city?"

"Yes, dear one," he replied. "In your world sacred space is toned down, for your bodies cannot handle such unrestrained presence in their current state."

"Why not?" asked Mason. "I mean, I know it sounds crazy, but I feel like I was made for this kind of space. Like this is all I ever wanted in life."

"Without a doubt, friend," said Sarx. "You were made for nothing less. Unfortunately, your bodies inherited a corruption over time that has made your entry into this space–well, for lack of a better word–*dangerous*."

"Dangerous?" the two said, desiring more detail.

"Indeed," Sarx responded. "Some have died just by getting too close to the sacred spaces that we've installed on the earth—and those sacred spaces are mere shadows of this one."

"Uh," paused Mason, his heart beating quickly. "Are we going to die here then?"

"No, no," laughed Sarx while shaking his head. "The bodies you have on now are not average bodies. In fact, your bodies have now become sacred space for the Spirit of Light to dwell in."

"So we're not human anymore?" asked Junia, while bashfully waving at an angel that was waving at her.

"Quite the contrary," replied Sarx. "If anything, you're almost more human than you once were—a step closer to what you were designed to be before the corruption took over. But you're also becoming something more than that, which you will see in time."

Sarx then put out his hand and stopped the siblings in their tracks, right in front of the most glorious garden they had ever seen in what seemed to be the center of the cube. They weren't sure how they had reached the center as the cube was enormous, but their expedient travel was hardly the strangest thing that had happened to them in the last 24 hours.

The garden was illuminated by the brightest light they had seen yet and it seemed to make everything around Mason and Junia more clear and more beautiful. Everything that the light touched had an unreal vibrancy to it, the colors exploding as though they themselves were alive. There were colors that Mason and Junia had never seen before that left their mouths agape.

Sarx then picked up in conversation where he left off. "Now just as the sacred spaces on land are shadows of this place, so are your current bodies shadows of the kind of body you will be given later when the time is right."

Mason and Junia wanted so badly to go into the garden. "When will that time be?" asked Junia, a longing cracking in her voice.

"I'm not sure, to be honest," replied Sarx. "I suspect soon, but in the Kingdom of Heaven, time is a bit of loaded concept. One day might go by here and yet a thousand years may have passed on earth. Whatever the case may be, I don't make the call on when the timing is right."

"Then who does?" asked Mason.

"The one whom your current bodies cannot yet approach," Sarx answered. "The Creator of all, whether it be Heaven or earth or physical or spiritual. Everything in existence, including you, comes from him."

"Is that light him?" asked Junia.

"Well, yes, that's what he looks like to you now. But when the fullness comes, you'll be able to see more than light–you'll be able to see him face to face!" There was such joy in Sarx's voice. "He has a plan to restore *all* things! And not just to restore it, but to make it better than it ever was!"

"The Creator will create again?" asked Mason.

"Well sure!" exclaimed Sarx. "Haven't you heard that the Creator rested after a long streak of creating?"

The siblings nodded.

"Then just imagine what he'll create when he's done resting!" Sarx smiled as his eyes teared up. "Just imagine," he whispered.

Sarx's wonderment brought a trickle to Junia's eyes. "King Sarx, forgive me for not understanding this, but you called this place Heaven?"

Sarx nodded, still gazing upon the garden, teary-eyed.

"I guess I don't understand," she continued. "I thought Heaven was—you know—up there? In the clouds?"

Sarx's posture was unfazed as he continued to stare into the sacred space in front of him. "Well dear one, the world of Heaven is often upside down from what humans expect." And then breaking out with a chuckle he said, "In fact, it's almost always the opposite of what humans expect."

"How can that be?" asked Mason. "There's pretty extensive speculation back home among the religious folk."

"Indeed there is, son," he responded. "But the corruption on the earth is strong—even among those who study the very prophets that we commissioned in this place. The corruption has a way of causing the religious to hear and read the prophets in an unloving light. They twist our prophetic words in the most despicable ways."

He then turned to look the two in their eyes. "Water and death are the path to Heaven. It is a place for the lowly—for those who have descended to the greatest depths and lived their lives as slaves for others. It may sound backwards, but that is the true path to glory, honor and power. But that is not the teaching of the corruption or those infected by it." Sarx noted an expression of fear upon the siblings' faces. "And the fact that this teaching makes you uneasy proves that your bodies are only shadows of what is to come. For when that time comes, even your thoughts will be aligned with

Heaven. But blessed are those who can grasp this teaching in their current state, for their toil and sweat and blood on behalf of the kingdom of Heaven might pave a path wide enough for even their enemies to walk."

The two remained silent for a moment, and then Mason broke in. "I'm sorry, I'm having a hard time understanding that," he said.

"Like I said," started Sarx, leaning close to Mason and tapping his forehead. "Heaven is often upside down to humans. The corruption still clouds your old mind and tries to affect your old skin. Don't think that just because you're a citizen here means your decisions will be correct for now on. Many of our residents have spread the corruption in the name of Heaven, and many will fall condemned for the portrait they have painted of this place and its king. You two mustn't do the same. You must understand that you can still fall prey to the corruption—for believe it or not, even some of the angels that once lived here gave into the corruption, turned against the Creator, and were sentenced to the earth."

"What?" gasped Junia. "Who would ever put the opportunity to live here on the line? It's everything anyone could ever dream of!"

"You would think that," said Sarx. "Yet even Heaven has seen its share of rebellions. And those rebellions became the seed of the corruption on the earth. In fact, an angel of light—*known on earth as the Plaintiff*—once guarded this very spot and sat in the presence of the Creator day by day."

"What happened?" asked Mason.

"Once the corruption came, his heart became hard and cold and he soon made the hearts of others here hard and cold as well. It spread like a disease. He plotted to usurp the Creator's throne and take over all creation."

"And did he?" asked Mason.

"Did he?" asked Sarx sharply with an instant fire in his eyes. "Son, the very fact that you would wonder shows that the corruption is still upon your thinking. How could the created overthrow the Uncreated? Simple logic undoes such ridiculous thinking. But pride is an arrogant beast that can overcome even the minds of those who were once among the Creator's best friends."

Sarx's perfect sense made Mason more than a little embarrassed and both Sarx and Junia noted it.

"But that's enough for now friends," Sarx said as his shoulders relaxed. "The two of you have learned more than most in a short walk."

"Are we leaving?" asked Junia.

"Only for a time," he responded. "You will see this place again down the road. And one day we will install it upon the earth after our full plans come to fruition. The Kingdom may start in the ocean, but it evaporates under pressure and is rained down throughout the whole earth–drop by drop, century by century. The Creator has a plan in place, and there is no stopping what he has set his mind to. And we are a part of that plan, for the Creator has chosen you two to serve alongside me."

"He's chosen us?" asked Junia.

"Well of course! Do you really think you could have gotten through the gates of Heaven by your own admission? " Sarx laughed. "The two of you will help me plant Heaven on the earth as I deal a deathblow to the corruption and the kingdom that lies behind its expansion. For since the Plaintiff was banned from Heaven and sent to the earth, he has done a massive amount of damage to the Creator's world. But I will ensure his end. For while he and his minions may currently be immortal, the Creator has a plan to end them once and for all along with sin and corruption and all the damage it has done to creation."

Sarx then looked deeply into Junia and Mason's eyes and asked, "Chosen ones: Will you join me?"

The two had never felt more important. They didn't fully understand who this Plaintiff was or what they were getting into, but they knew they had to help. They could choose not to, of course, but to do so seemed to say no to destiny.

They looked to each other and then back to Sarx. "We're in," said Mason.

"Good," Sarx smiled. "Then let's be on our way. Though first, let me check on some old friends."

# CHAPTER 7
## Old Friends

Sarx's fist knocked against the door three times in an authoritative, yet gentle way. The three were now in another district within the kingdom that was full of large houses for as far as the eye could see. The door opened quickly.

"King Sarx! Old friend!" exclaimed the glowing being inside as he opened the door hurriedly. He appeared to be more like a man than an angel, but he also seemed to have an angelic shimmer upon him.

"What an honor!" said the man excitedly. "Come in, come in. How are you? Can I get you a drink? Some of our best wine perhaps?"

"That would be lovely, Morales, but unfortunately I'm on a fast from Kingdom drink till my mission has reached its full end," smiled Sarx.

"Ah, of course," said Morales as he pointed his finger in remembrance. "Well I suppose the abstinence will make that particular cup taste all the sweeter! It will most certainly be drunk during a celebration to remember I imagine."

"*Thee* celebration," winked Sarx.

"Ah yes–*thee* celebration," smirked Morales, pointing his finger once again. "How about some water then?"

"Brother, you tempt me!" laughed Sarx.

"Oh dear!" said Morales as he gazed upward and put his hand on his forehead. "Forgive me Master Sarx. I forget what it's like to wear such skin. I suppose the waters here would prove too dangerous for you yet."

"Only if certain death sounds '*too dangerous*' to you," laughed Sarx as they stepped into the large house.

"Well, it wouldn't be the first time I've faced that beast," chuckled Morales. The siblings eyebrows were raised high as they tried to dissect the conversation into understandable pieces. Morales saw their expression and tried to clarify. "I mean death. *That* foul beast."

Mason swallowed hard and tried to choke out a few words. "You–you've faced death?"

"Most of our kind here have," answered a voice from behind Morales. Morales moved out of the way and Mason and Junia gazed upon another being like him that was sitting on a couch in the living room sipping tea.

"You mean, like 99.999% of our kind," Morales laughed boisterously as he took a drink of water. He tried to continue talking before he had swallowed it all. "Allow me to introduce you to Vox. *He's undead!*" he said with a spooky voice as he moved his fingers slowly through the air.

"You know that joke drives me crazy old man!" said Vox in a joking tone that also carried a bit of annoyance.

"Old man is right sonny!" Morales smiled as he waved an imaginary cane at Vox and added some vibrato to his voice. "So old that I had to face death itself to get here!"

"That's not the legends they tell of you on earth these days," said Vox.

"Yes, yes, I've heard," laughed Morales. "Can't have a hero go dying anymore. Everyone always has to come up with some rumor of how they cheated death." He took another drink and then looked at the siblings again as he swallowed. "But in his case, it's actually true! Would you believe that Heaven sent him his own little trolley to pick him up?"

Mason and Junia had heard of such a story before, but it had always sounded a bit preposterous.

"Yep," continued Morales. "He jumped right on in and caught a free ride straight to Heaven."

Vox sighed heavily as though annoyed. But then, glancing up at Sarx he admitted, "It was pretty awesome."

"Vox the Undead!" exclaimed Sarx in a triumphant tone as he put out his arms.

"Vox the Undead!" responded Vox in equal measure as he got off the couch and gave Sarx a hug. "Master, it is good to see you."

"The same, brother," replied Sarx.

"Ditto," agreed Morales as he added a third wheel of a hug into the mix.

"Personal space old man!" laughed Vox.

Morales let go and laughed. "You young whipper-snappers!"

Sarx then looked to the siblings who looked as confused as ever. "Morales. Vox. I'd like to introduce to my friends, Mason and Junia."

"Wonderful choice in names King Sarx," said Vox. "It'll serve them well."

"What does that mean?" asked Mason as the two took their place on the living room furniture.

"In due time friends," smiled Sarx. "In due time."

"I feel there's a lot we need to become clear of in due time," laughed Junia. "I'm not sure I've understood much of anything the last few days."

"Oh, I'm sure this has been quite a wild ride for you two," said Morales. "Allow me to clear the air a little bit. You may have heard about me in the sacred book. I am Morales, keeper of the Creator's wisdom. 'Twas my job on Earth, 'tis my job in Heaven. Though as you can see," he said, gesturing to the library behind him, "I've expanded a bit on his wisdom since getting here."

"You wrote all of those books?" said Junia, her mouth wide open.

"Indeed!" Morales smiled. "And more libraries shall I write in time!"

Mason's stomach dropped like a stone inside him as the sinful memories from his watery journey played through his head once more. These numerous holy books felt like pure condemnation.

"See, a long time ago, we were just innocent beings, living innocent lives in the Creator's presence. It was a beautiful place—really no place like it has been on Earth since," said Morales.

"Though one greater is coming," interjected Sarx.

"Oh yes, very much so," agreed Morales. "And when that time comes our ability to meet God's standards will be here in full as well! But only the Creator knows when that time is coming. Until then, the beings on earth live in the In-Between."

"The In-Between?" asked Junia.

"Yes," answered Morales. "The In-Between. For earthly beings are no longer the innocent beings they once were, nor are they yet the perfect beings they one day will be. If they were innocent in their thinking, they could hardly be accused of sin even if they did, in fact, sin. But that phase of spiritual history has long passed and all of humanity now lives in the In-Between."

"What brought about the In-Between?" asked Mason, his stomach in knots.

"Ah, that would be the Plaintiff," interjected Vox.

"You mentioned him before, King Sarx," said Junia. "Who is he exactly?"

"Yes, well, as I mentioned, the Plaintiff used to be a citizen here," replied Sarx. "And like all the citizens here, he was a being of light who was actually pretty far up the chain of command—an appointed guardian who watched over the Creator's presence. He had much to be desired by many: Wisdom. Beauty. He was quite perfect–blameless in his decisions. That is, until the corruption was found in him."

"Oh the violence," said Vox, his words muffled by his fist over his mouth.

"What made him change?" asked Junia.

"Well, like many still today, the Plaintiff was corrupted by that which was good in him," explained Sarx.

"How does that work?" asked Mason.

"Like I said, he was a thing of beauty to behold. I mean, who wouldn't be alluring with such wisdom and righteousness? Does one really need anything else to be found attractive?" Sarx questioned. "Of course, couple that beauty with pride and you're left with a dangerous mixed drink."

"And that's how something good became something bad," said Morales. "Though he lived in the presence of God, his focus became on himself. He started to think he was better and wiser than him."

"And that's how you go from image to idol," interjected Vox.

"Exactly," agreed Morales.

"What do you mean?" asked Junia.

Morales let out a long sigh. "Human beings and spiritual beings alike are made in the Creator's image and thus it is our job to be *imagers*–in other words, we show the earth and the Heavens what God is like in all of his ways. But an image of God turned in on itself becomes what many these days call an idol. And an idol goes from worshipping God to worshipping itself. It becomes a false image of God because it no longer mirrors him."

"So that which is made *like* God begins to think that it *is* God?" said Junia with intrigue in her voice.

"Precisely," said Morales. "But much of mankind fails to see such a simple truth time and time again."

"You mentioned there was violence?" interjected Mason.

"Yes, a rebellion in Heaven," said Sarx. "I spoke to you briefly of it earlier. The Plaintiff's pride was so great that he actually tried to usurp the throne of the one-and-only Creator and take control of the Heavenly Council."

"If he could get control of that, he would then rule all the beings in the spiritual and physical world," explained Vox.

"But he could never do that," said Mason. "As you said earlier, it's simple logic. How could the created destroy the Uncreated?"

"Indeed," said Sarx.

"It's pure arrogance my boy," said Morales as he reclined in his chair. "To think that you have more power than the very source of power itself? Ridiculous! And yet that is the kind of thinking that happens when an image becomes an idol."

"But you said he was full of wisdom. How could he be that stupid?" asked Mason.

"Well, just think of the wisest people you've ever met on earth," said Vox. "Is it not some of the wisest people you know who have done some of the stupidest things you've ever seen?"

"Right. Wisdom doesn't make a person infallible," said Morales. Then looking directly at Sarx he said, "After all, wisdom–*true wisdom anyways*–is a person, not a character trait. And all wisdom outside of that person is, I suppose, stupidity in contrast."

"Yet human beings are not the only people to chase after false wisdom en masse," said Vox. "The Plaintiff managed to convince a hefty number of Heavenly beings to join him."

"About a third of the ranks here," added Sarx.

"What happened to them?" asked Junia.

"Well you met Miguel already, yes?" asked Morales. "Big guy? Fearsome to behold?"

Junia and Mason's hearts plummeted at the very memory. They nodded slowly.

"Yes, well, Miguel and his own army of angels rose up against the Plaintiff and kicked him and his angels out of the kingdom of Heaven and banished them to the earth," explained Morales. "It's great news for us!–but, of course, bad news for humanity. He now burns with a hatred like never before and he has a taste for blood and vengeance. The corruption has taken him over fully. He is a god unto himself and he knows no other. He is an idol and the face behind the movement that lies behind every idol on earth. He sees a million little images of the Creator running around and he wants to snuff them out for his own false glory."

"Not to mention that he loves to watch the image of God suffer," added Vox. "Every time a human pursues hatred over love, he knows he has sent a personal attack to the Creator. And the more humans fight to remain the Creator's imager, the more greatly the Plaintiff and his minions attack them.

He'll kill them if he has to–and he has! Since the very moment he touched earth he has been seeking to steal, kill and destroy."

"The picture you're painting seems a little extravagant for a Plaintiff," said Mason. "I mean, isn't that like a legal term or something? Or is that his name?"

"He does not deserve a name, for he is not and will not be," replied Sarx. "Therefore, you are given an accurate description of what he does–a noun to remember him by. He is a plaintiff. You are correct, it's a legal term. He uses his wisdom to make cases against humanity in attempts to condemn them before the Creator. Day and night, he accuses people, longing for wrath to be poured out upon them."

"Does it work?" asked Junia. "I mean, does the Creator listen?"

"No, but your kind certainly does," replied Morales. "A fair amount of the depression humans battle is the belief that they are accused, guilty and condemned. The Plaintiff has corrupted everything to communicate that to them–even good things!"

"Like what?" asked Mason.

"Well as I mentioned earlier," continued Morales, "I was known on the earth for the documentation of God's standards. It was important work to do because the first thing the Plaintiff did when he met the early humans was trick them into pursuing 'so-called wisdom' outside of the Creator. This, of course, is foolishness, *for the Creator is wisdom itself.*"

"This pursuit had many consequences," added Vox. "For one, humanity was exposed to the corruption and has been diseased with it ever since. Secondly, we had to be removed from the most intimate spaces of the Creator's presence. And thirdly–*and most importantly to our current discussion*–we gained the knowledge of that which is good and that which is bad."

"Right," nodded Morales. "And since there was no going back–no returning to a time of innocence where sin wasn't sin–it was important to document a certain rule for living; that is, that which is good and pleasing to God, and that which is bad and should be avoided and repented of."

"Yet these legal rule books of God's standards were to some extent corrupted by the Plaintiff, because who knows legality better than him?" Vox shrugged.

"Exactly," said Morales. "The heart behind the rules was good. But the way in which the Plaintiff twisted the rules was bad. A good lawyer always knows how to play the game and he constantly throws out accusations by twisting the heart and intention of God's wisdom."

"Just think of life as you know it right now," interjected Vox. "Right now there are countless people quoting Morales' Godly work with hearts of hatred and oppression, which is the work of the Plaintiff, not of the loving Creator."

"Yes, and that's just the six hundred or so laws I wrote in that time–a shadow of the real law, so I've discovered. Obviously, the library behind me shows that there are far greater depths and truer expressions of the Creator's wisdom than what I originally wrote. A being of infinite goodness and wisdom requires an infinite amount of libraries."

Morales then paused as a tear swelled up in his eyes. "The things I've learned about how he loves–even heavenly paper can hardly contain it. Such words always bleed through the pages and make such a mess of things." Morales then drifted off into space for a moment, before returning to the conversation. "I'm sorry, where was I?" he asked.

"Did you forget old man?" smirked Vox.

"Oh you young people these days!" laughed Morales as he threw his hands up in the air. "You *undead* young people these days!" Vox shook his head.

"So when we get back to Earth, should we be looking for a lawyer?" asked Mason.

The three laughed so loudly at the question that they began to tear up.

"What's so funny?" asked Junia.

"I'm gathering we all just got the same image in our mind," laughed Vox.

"Right," said Morales, wiping his eyes. "A huge dragon wearing a suit and tie and carrying a bunch of legal documents around!" They burst into laughter again.

"A dragon?" gulped Junia.

"Yes," said Sarx, his cheeks still burning from the laughter. "It's not quite what he looked like when he was here. The corruption has taken him over rather fully–that is to say, all that is *not* God has taken him over. He's almost like anti-creation, if you will. Pure chaos. And chaos has a certain look to it."

"I only know of one dragon on earth," said Mason. "Is he the infamous Dragon of the South?"

"The same," said Sarx. "He tried to ascend high into the skies to reign over creation, so he was sentenced to the ground where he reigns over dirt. He was booted out of the Heavens; away from the heavenly courtroom; away from the divine throne; out of the sacred holy presence; and his body made a crater in the mountains upon impact. The Creator had his legs removed from him as a fitting reminder of his sentence. He is now so low that he cannot even stand up–he trips over his own face."

"You could even say he's lower than that," added Morales. "He's been sentenced to below the earth—the realm of the dead."

"But isn't that you?" asked Mason. Morales looked at him with a raised eyebrow. "Sorry, what I mean is, aren't you dead?"

"Ah, I see," replied Morales. "So, those who remain faithful to God and image him are welcomed by God into Heaven. So though I may have died, I still entered into glory."

"Glory? Is that why you're glowing the way you are?" asked Mason.

"Indeed," he answered.

"Also, by logical deduction, the opposite is true," added Vox. "Become an idol for the corruption and Heaven becomes closed to you. Those who die in the corruption, pass into the death it brings, and are subjected to the Plaintiff's rule; for he holds the keys to death and the underworld."

"So simply put, good people go to Heaven and bad people don't?" asked Junia.

"No dear, it's much more complicated than that," Sarx chimed in. "The day will come when all throughout history will be judged before the Creator. There will be some that get in that you wouldn't expect. And on the opposite side, there will be some who think they will get through our gates with no problem, yet they'll find themselves with worse judgment than those they thought condemned."

"I'm having a hard time following the formula as to who gets in and who doesn't," said Junia as she grasped her forehead.

"Simply put, the Creator is the ultimate judge on that," Sarx clarified. "Just as Morales has his own library here, so does the Creator have one. It's filled to the brim with books about every last human, each book attesting to the life that they lived. Nothing has been missed and so no judgment could be more accurate and more final. In his omniscience the Creator's declarations are perfectly just."

"Though King Sarx plays an essential role in this too," Vox pointed out.

"True," nodded Sarx. "For the Creator has plans to make me the jury for all of these trials. And though his books will incriminate everyone, he and I have decided that those who appeal to me while alive on earth will have their sins forgiven and allowed entrance into Heaven, regardless of what they've done. Their sins will be completely erased from their book."

Mason suddenly felt a relief from the pressure he felt earlier. He now understood why Morales was so easily moved to tears when he talked about God's love. With a smile he asked, "And all of those people who get in, they'll glow in glory like you guys?"

"Yes," replied Morales. "Granted, how you see us now is how we look in the In-Between. At the end of all things we have been promised that we will return to physical bodies that will be superior to our previous ones in every way. And they will be very glorious. But for now we are simply glorious spirits."

"You kind of look a lot like the angels here," said Junia. "I mean, you glow like them anyways."

"Well, whether we be human spirits or angelic spirits, all the host of Heaven can be classified as 'holy ones,'" said Vox. "You might even consider we human spirits to be the replacement plan for the Plaintiff and his minions. We are the new holy ones meant to replace the old fallen holy ones; the newly redeemed and adopted earthly family replacing the old fallen and disinherited heavenly family."

"Replacement?" asked Mason. "Would we be doing the work that the fallen holy ones used to do here then?"

"Yes!" exclaimed Morales with excitement. "Heavenly beings have always played a part in making judgment calls, ruling with authority, and executing the Creator's will. From what I can tell, the Creator intends to extend those responsibilities to us. Though we were born human, we will one day go so far as to judge angels themselves!"

"I guess I'm a little confused again," said Junia. "You just said that the Creator and King Sarx were the ones who judged and ruled. How do humans or angels fit into that role as well?"

"There is only one Creator, child," responded Vox. "He is the one and only God and all that exists—whether it be spiritual or physical—exists because he made it. That being said, by all means the Creator could do whatever he wants to do. He has all the power, all the wisdom, all the glory, and is present in all places at all times. He does not need us. And yet for reasons perhaps too complicated to fully understand, he has decided to co-labor with other beings he has made to get his work done. Surely this has to do with his capacity to love, but it nonetheless remains a mystery.

"Indeed," agreed Morales. "He's even gone so far as to assign some of the upper-level spiritual beings here the power to rule over nations of people on the earth," said Vox.

"What?" exclaimed Mason. "No, that can't be right. That would make them—"

"Gods?" replied Vox. "Right."

"But you just said that there is only one God," Mason shot back.

"It would be heresy to believe anything else," replied Vox. "There is only one God. One Creator. Holy and set apart from all things. Yet in his desire to co-labor, he has assigned other beings he created to reign over different nations. They have many names on the earth: Principalities, powers, demons—and yes, they even get called the 'little-g-gods.' They are not God—not by a long shot—but they also aren't nothing. They take reign over all kinds of countries."

"But the stories on earth of those gods are dark," Junia said, cutting Vox off. "*Like, real dark*. They sound like total corruption."

"That's because they are," said Morales. "If they had done their job right, they would have filled themselves with the image of the Creator. But instead, they too became idols and turned their followers into hosts of the corruption. They, like the Plaintiff, have chosen anti-creation over creation; sin over righteousness; hatred over love; self over God. They are in leagues with the Dragon of the South, and they are all busy scheming and destroying."

"You'd think the Creator would just do things himself from this point on," laughed Vox. "But after he ends all of these fallen powers once and for all, he's mentioned that he plans to distribute reign throughout the kingdom, even to human holy ones."

"And are you human, King Sarx?" asked Mason. The room fell quiet as everyone waited for an answer. There was silence for some time before Sarx replied.

"What do you see before you?" asked Sarx.

"A man, I think," replied Mason. "I mean, you don't have the shape of one of the heavenly beings, nor do you glow like Morales or Vox in their current glory. You look like… well, like us."

"Yet you're the King of Heaven," interjected Junia. "And that seems to imply that you're not human?"

Suddenly a cloud began to fill the room and Sarx's face and clothes lit up to a level of brightness that was incomparable with either Morales, Vox, or any of the angels they had met. Everyone in the room had to cover their eyes for fear of going blind–yet at the same time they had never felt that going blind could be more worth a quick look. Mason and Junia felt as though they were staring at the same light that the Creator had radiated in the garden at the center of the kingdom.

Suddenly a voice like thunder cracked across the room, shaking everyone to their core. "Listen to my Son," it proclaimed boldly. The room then quickly returned to the way it had been a moment ago.

"Does that answer your question?" asked Sarx.

"I have no idea," replied Mason, his eyes as wide open as could be.

# CHAPTER 8
## Leaving Home

"Where are we going now?" asked Junia as they waved goodbye to Morales and Vox. She sensed they were headed back to the city entrance, but she didn't wish to leave yet. She had very much enjoyed her time in the Water Kingdom and wanted to stay much longer, if not indefinitely.

"We have work to do now," said Sarx. "Those who enter the waters of Heaven as one being, exit them as another–*and they always exit.*"

"I wouldn't mind skipping that part," chuckled Mason. "Home has nothing for us in comparison to this place. We could just stay here."

"Well what good would that serve the mission?" laughed Sarx. "If all of our human citizens were to just make the voyage over here, who would be left on the earth to image the Creator? Who would be left to show the world what it means to be truly human? Who would keep the corruption at bay? A world without true imagers? Now that would be a very dark place indeed."

## LEAVING HOME

"Is that part of our role in your mission?" asked Mason.

"A part," Sarx replied as the three approached the gate. "Granted, imaging God on the earth has always been your mission as a human being—it's built into your very core as an imager. Now, however, as a new creation with the Spirit of Light inside of you, you've been enabled to carry out the image in a greater capacity than you would have been able to carry by your own strength. And having passed through the waters of death, you will now emerge as new beings—though you won't look it. Here in the In-Between, you will find much of the new creation on the inside of you, where the Spirit works—where your spirit and the Spirit of Light mingle and play."

"So we'll be perfect imagers then?" asked Junia.

Sarx laughed. "Not quite daughter. But you'll be empowered to become what might be considered perfect during the time of the In-Between. The Spirit will require that you grow—*a lot*. And as always, growth takes time, effort, and comes with its fair share of pain as well. He will teach you to strip off what is left of the old creation in you so that you might grow into the new creation you've been empowered to be. You will exit the waters clean of corruption, but not immune to it. You will also exit the waters wholly allegiant to the Water Kingdom—*that is, the Kingdom of Heaven*. You now hold citizenship there, and so you must live a Heavenly life while on the earth."

Miguel turned from his post to see Sarx and the siblings. He smiled and nodded their direction. "Leaving so soon?" his voiced bellowed, a certain sadness in his expression.

"Unfortunately so, good friend," replied Sarx. "Though with the Spirit's help we'll be back."

"It is sad to see you go Master," said Miguel. "But I know that you, too, have a mission to carry out. I also know that should you request it, the Creator will send me and my entire army to your side." Miguel put his fist to his chest and bowed his head.

"I appreciate that, Miguel," smiled Sarx. "But that is not the plan. Though I did appreciate the help of the few angels my Father sent me last week after the trials I endured."

Miguel nodded in understanding. He then pulled out a horn from inside his robe and blew it with incredible intensity. Spirits from all across the city, appeared quickly, almost as though they had warped to their very location. They filled the streets of the Water Kingdom for as far as the eye could see.

"King Sarx is leaving us for now," proclaimed Miguel. "Let him depart with a blessing!"

The multitude responded in unison. "Glory to God in the highest, and on earth, peace among those with whom he is pleased!"

A smirk took over Sarx's face. He then looked to the wall of water at the gate, knit his brow, and took on the stance of a runner ready to take off. "Glory to God!" he yelled.

"Glory to God!" the beings returned.

"And peace," he whispered to himself closing his eyes. He then took off as fast as he could and dived head first into the wall of water, leaving the host of Heaven staring at Mason and Junia who had clearly missed their chance to leave in such an epic manner.

"Uh," stumbled Mason as he and his sister backed up slowly towards the wall of water. "I guess we'll be going too–" The word *"too"* became an elongated screech of sorts as Sarx's arm came out of the wall of water, wrapped around them, and yanked them backwards into it.

# CHAPTER 9
## SEA MONSTER

The three rose through the waters at incredible speed, almost as though something was propelling them upward. Yet despite their pace, they still had a long way to go.

*Did it take us this long to reach the ocean floor?* they wondered. How long had they been lost in their memories on the way down?

The sun shimmered through the ocean surface as rays of light began to illuminate the waters around them. It would only be a few more minutes before they reached the top now. The frigid waters grew warmer by the second.

And then suddenly colder. Their supernatural speed came to an immediate stop as Sarx looked left and right with a cautious expression on his face. "Watch yourselves," he warned the two.

# SEA MONSTER

Junia and Mason spun in circles in attempts to see what Sarx was talking about, but saw nothing. Then suddenly the light above them went dark. They were afraid to look up. *What on earth could be large enough to block that much sunlight?* they thought.

"It's not *from* earth," Sarx replied, as though he could hear their thoughts. The darkness then closed in around them until the sun was no more. The oceans fell completely silent. Even the sound of the rushing tide went silent. Then a thunderous, low-pitched noise filled their ears, as though a being of massive size had just groaned–the water being warmed by its breath.

"Ssssson of God," it said with a disturbing hiss.

As those words were spoken the siblings beheld a small glimpse of the monster, for its mouth was full of bright flames that were somehow unextinguished by the sea. The creature was absolutely enormous, their bodies about the size of its pupil. The being gave a devilish smirk as fire came out the sides of its mouth.

Mason and Junia looked around them and saw nothing but reptilian scales, each seeming to move as the being's body twisted and contorted. They could now discern that this giant sea serpent had spun around them enough times to encapsulate the three of them inside a sphere-like shape. They had no way out. "Ssssson of God," he repeated slowly, the flames pouring out of his mouth. "What purpose do you have here? Sssssurely it is not time for the end of all things already."

"Don't be mistaken, Levi. There is indeed a sword in Heaven with your name on it," threatened Sarx. Junia and Mason glanced at each other in fear– partially because of the giant being before them, but also because their tiny little leader had just threatened this incredible beast. It wouldn't take much to kill them.

"Sssssso it's been written," Levi replied with a growl. "Yet I do not sssssee any sssssword now." A creepy smile took over the serpent's face.

"That's because you're a creature of chaos and you think my sword looks like an actual sword," said Sarx.

Levi bellowed a deep laugh from his gut, which, when you're a snake, is a very deep laugh indeed. It came out of him in surround sound, shaking the three around in the water. "I am not a creature of chaos—*I am chaosssss*," he declared. "And I will turn the Creator's finely ordered world into chaos as well! It will become a world in which all are free to live however they want. A world in which every man livesssss for himsssssself. There he will take whatever he desires and love however he definessss it."

"That's anarchy!" replied Sarx.

"That'sssss freedom," Levi roared, the flames rising out the sides of his mouth higher than before.

"No," said Sarx boldly. "The only freedom you will ever find is deep within the order the Creator has put in place. Anarchy isn't freedom—it's bondage. And it will be your downfall. You are a time bomb waiting to go off. For what lives in chaos, finds its end in chaos."

"Sssssspoken like the true Sssssson of God," Levi hissed. "Did your Daddy teach you that?"

Sarx knit his brow once again. "You would be wise to heed my word, Levi. For my sword is my mouth. With a word you were brought into creation, and with a word you will be taken out of it, along with everything else that brings chaos and corruption upon the earth."

## SEA MONSTER

The serpent's pupils shrunk as fire sprang from his mouth and nostrils alongside a low growl.

"Now let us pass so you do not need to experience a foreshadowing of what I will do to you later," Sarx continued, staring directly into Levi's eyes.

Suddenly the beast closed his mouth and the waters fell pitch black once more. Mason looked around frantically, waiting to see if they were being let go or not.

"I will establisssssh CHAOSSSSSS," the snake roared as he opened his mouth and began to pour out fire upon the three. The flames reached incredible intensity and Mason and Junia were sure their lives were over. But suddenly the serpent yelped and uncoiled, for his body had caught fire. The creature had become so enraged at Sarx's words that he had forgotten he was unleashing fire upon his own body. He uncoiled from his sphere-like shape and spread his enormous body out across the sea for what looked like miles.

"This isn't over Ssssson of God," he bellowed as he swam away, his singed scales continuing to smoke.

Sarx then grabbed Junia and Mason by the hand and blasted off towards the surface, gathering so much momentum that they actually burst out the ocean nearly 20 feet into the sky. They unexpectedly gasped for air, forgetting what it was like to need breath inside of them. It was like being punched in the gut. They braced themselves as they came plummeting back towards a large wave, but rather than fall through it, they found themselves sliding down the back side of it. Sarx stood up quickly on the waters and wrenched out his cloak.

"How did we survive that fire?" exclaimed Mason.

"Forget that! How are we standing on the ocean?" asked Junia as she pulled herself up to her knees.

Sarx bent over as he continued to adjust to the notion of breathing again. "Yes, yes, very good questions," he said. "Mason—just so you know—that was not the first time in history that a son of God survived a fire with no problem. And Junia, you'll find that chaos has no control over me unless I let it." He coughed out some water and chuckled. "I walk on chaos' face."

Mason also coughed out some water as he rose to his feet. "Perhaps this isn't the time for more questions, but there are other sons of God? You're not the only one?" he asked, bending over and grabbing his chest.

"Think back to what Morales and Vox were saying," answered Sarx. "There is only one God, right?"

"Right," the two answered, as water dripped off their hair into their face.

"Yet at the same time, there are other beings that God has created that—*though they are nothing like God*—still carry the title of little-g-gods," he explained. "The term 'son of God' is a phrase that has been used throughout the ages to describe powerful spiritual beings."

"I think I see where you're headed," said Junia. "So in the same way that there are many 'gods,' but really only one true God—technically there are also many 'sons of God,' though really only one true Son of God, which is you, of course. The real deal, set apart and different from the others."

"I think we have a budding theologian on our hands!" smiled Sarx as Junia blushed. "Yes, you are correct. However, it's important you guys keep that to yourselves for now. You can reveal your revelations in due time. Really, everything you've experienced in the last few hours needs to be kept to yourselves until the time is right."

# SEA MONSTER

"All this time I thought you were human," said Mason. "Well, I mean, kind of human. I don't know, I feel like I'm getting mixed signals."

Sarx laughed. "Understandable. Our next stop should help you sort that out a bit more."

Mason looked around and saw nothing but sun for miles. "And where exactly is that next stop?"

Sarx turned in a circle as though to look for something. He put his hand above his eyes to shield them from the sun and squinted hard. "Ah, there it is," he said.

"What is?" asked Mason.

"Our ride," he smiled.

"What?" the two asked together.

"Not all massive sea creatures are disobedient to the throne," explained Sarx. "This one has actually been loyal for some time."

Suddenly the top half of an enormous mouth came rising out of the sea around them, causing Mason and Junia to realize that the strange texture touching their backs must have been a massive tongue. The mouth slammed shut with a boom, trapping them inside.

They each rolled to a different place in the mouth. It was a bit disturbing to be sure, but at the same time, Mason and Junia couldn't help but smile and laugh.

"Hope you brought some games!" Sarx yelled jokingly across the beast's mouth. "We have a three day journey ahead of us. A journey not entirely unlike one I'll need to take later." Sarx then kindly patted the beast's tongue as though to say thank you and it let out a deep joyful noise.

# CHAPTER 10
## The Shore

"Run! Quick! Get out of the water!" screamed a lady from the shore. "There's something out there!"

The whole beach was thrown into a panic as people screamed and trudged to shore as quickly as they could. They could see a huge hump of water moving towards them at great speed–though the closer the hump got to the shore, the more the swimmers noticed that it seemed to be avoiding them. And then, as it reached the shallows, everyone laid eyes on the biggest fish you could ever imagine.

The fish was close to the shore, though not so close that he was beached–his eyes searching the crowd staring intently back at him. Most of the beach-goers stood on the shore at this point, but a few were still in the waters and were now approaching the great fish out of curiosity. Slowly, he began to open his giant mouth, causing them to jump back.

"What is that thing?" yelled a father from the sand.

"There's a man inside!" exclaimed a mother.

"And two others!" pointed another.

Sarx squinted as they all exited the fish. "Well, I won't be showing any interest in seafood for awhile," he said as the fish's giant mouth closed. He patted him on the nose. "Thank you friend. You have been more helpful in serving the Creator than many of the humans I know."

The great fish let out a strange noise of affection and–*if possible*–seemed to express a dull grin. He then began to flop around until he had managed to get himself back into the deep and take off. The three of them watched as he departed and then turned around to find a crowd full of gaping mouths and wide eyes staring at them in silence.

"Good morning!" greeted Sarx. Then, looking up to the sky and seeing the sun's position, he said, "I mean, good afternoon!

The crowd remained silent.

Suddenly there was a tug on his shirt and he turned to see a small child with an eyepatch standing next to him. "Are you good, sir?" he boldly asked.

Sarx kneeled down to get on his level. "*I am,*" he responded. Then pointing at the boy's eyepatch, he said, "Are you?"

The boy blushed and glanced away in shame. "It's not polite to stare, sir," he said.

"Oh son," replied Sarx. "You've been this way since birth. It wasn't anything you did. There's nothing to be ashamed about."

A look of confusion came over the boy as the crowd looked on. "Do I know you?" he asked.

"No. But I know you," Sarx smiled. "Tell me son, would you like to see?"

The boy looked to the shore and saw his mom frantically gesturing to him to come to her. He turned back to Sarx.

"What kind of question is that?" he responded.

"A simple one," Sarx smiled. "And one that not all sick people are able to answer honestly."

"Well I can," said the boy as he took on a firmer posture. "Of course I would like to see."

Sarx reached into the water and pulled up some wet sand. "May I?" he asked, pointing at the boy's eyepatch.

"Uh… sure?" said the boy. He had no idea what was going on, but at the same time, this man did just walk out of a giant fish. It seemed like a day for a miracle if ever there was one.

"Zamerion, get back here right now!" yelled the boy's mother as she began to walk towards Sarx.

Sarx lifted up the eyepatch and found a closed eyelid. He pulled the bottom half down to reveal that there was nothing inside. He spit into the sand in his hand and then fashioned the sand into a ball which somehow managed to hold its shape.

# THE SHORE

"Zamerion, get away from that man!" his mother yelled, the sound of her feet trudging loudly through the water. Sarx remained unfazed, his attention entirely on the boy.

Using his thumb and his pointer finger, Sarx opened the boy's eyelids and shoved the ball of sand inside.

"Get away from him you monster!" the woman screamed as she swept Zamerion up into her arms. She bounced the boy on her hip, his head on her shoulder. "Are you okay, baby?"

She then heard the silent weeping of her child, his chest heaving on her side.

"Baby? What's wrong?" She set him down on his feet and fell to her knees in the water to get a good look at his face. "What did he do to you baby? Open your eyes—let me see."

Then she gasped and threw her hand over her mouth. For she noticed that tears were flowing from not one, but both of Zamerion's eyelids.

"Mama," her son said, shaking. "I can see." He opened his eyelids to reveal two irritated and teary eyes. "Mama, I can see."

His mother wept as she placed her hands on the sides of his face in wonder. She let out the most terrible yet touching cry—the kind that shakes your body as it exits your nose—followed by a high-pitched inhale.

Junia and Mason stood amazed as Sarx knelt down in the water and put his hand on her shoulder. The woman, twisted around and grabbed Sarx's cloak and pulled him close so that her head rested on his chest. It was the kind of unsymmetrical embrace one can only give when they are beside themselves. She managed to whisper, "Thank you," as her tears added to the ocean waters. The boy joined in the hug and let out his own tears and thankfulness.

After a few more moments the woman sniffed heavily and stood to her feet. She then picked up her son once more as the crowd stared and murmured. Suddenly, a troop of about six officers showed up on horseback. Each jumped off their steeds quickly and approached the waters just in time to hear the woman laugh, "He can see! My son can see! He was born blind, and yet this man has done a miracle!" The crowd gasped and erupted with cheering as she pushed her face against the boy's cheek and smiled. "That means no more doctor visits, baby!"

The officers looked at each other, confused as to what they had just walked in on. The captain hushed the crowd and walked boldly out into the water. Mason and Junia hid behind Sarx. The woman also looked nervous of what was about to happen and prepared herself to come to Sarx's defense.

"Can I get your name, sir?" asked the captain.

"Sarx," he replied with a look of intrigue.

The captain fell to his knees into the water, shocking all his officers on the beach. They reached for their swords as though the action was so out of character for him that he must have fallen prey to some kind of magic.

"Please, Master Sarx," he pleaded. "I've tried everything–*everything*. My house is filled with hospital bills. My roommate has fallen deathly sick and there's nothing left that I can do for him. He's bound to pass any moment now–the doctor seemed sure it would be today. Please, if you can heal someone with a birth defect, surely you can heal someone who inherited a sickness along the way."

All the captain could see was Sarx's legs as he humbled himself before him. Then Sarx's outstretched hand entered his view, offering him to grab it. The officer took it slowly as Sarx pulled him to his feet and then placed his hands on his shoulders.

# THE SHORE

"Take me to him," said Sarx.

The captain's face lit up, but then immediately fell.

"What's wrong?" asked Sarx.

"Please sir," he replied. "You have performed the ways of the Creator today in front of all to see. You are far too good to enter a house like mine. Surely you can heal him from here?"

"You think so?" asked Sarx.

"Well sure," replied the Captain. "I mean, I don't have the kind of authority you have that I might command eyes to see, but I have the kind of authority to command my officers. Whatever I say, they do–they have to. And your authority is obviously far greater than mine! So please, heal him now–from here."

A smirk filled Sarx's face as his eyes opened wide. "Now *that* is faith," he said. "Very well. Your friend is healed. Go home and see for yourself!"

"Oh thank you, thank you!" smiled the captain as he splashed through the water toward the shore. "You give this man whatever he needs!" he said to his troop as he pointed at Sarx. He then hopped on his horse and took off as the crowd grew larger.

"I imagine there are some other requests here today," Sarx called out from his place in the waters. "I only ask one thing before we begin: I really want to be on land before we start."

The crowd let out a small laugh as Sarx nodded to his two partners and headed towards the shore. "Have them form a line," he instructed Mason and Junia. "Hope you're feeling rested. We're going to be here for awhile."

# CHAPTER 11
## THE FAMILY

The sun began to set as the world's longest line began to reach its end. Sarx had to be growing tired. He had been standing on his feet for hours, praying for countless people. Junia and Mason had seen him do miracle after miracle after miracle. Some came to him with minor problems like headaches and they disappeared in a moment. Others came to him with major problems like broken legs and lesions all over the body, and he healed those things too. People who hadn't walked in decades began to walk. Sores fell off of people onto the ground and disintegrated, leaving the smoothest, clearest skin you had ever seen.

And just as Sarx had casted a demon out of Kahli, so he had done to many in the line. In fact, sometimes he healed people by casting out demons. There were moments where he would identify people's sickness as a *spirit* of sorts and then he'd tell it to leave. It was becoming clear that some people's problems were natural while other's were supernatural–and perhaps other's were a blend of the two. It didn't matter what problem people had for Sarx to fix, he was able to take care of it all. Sure, one time he had to pray twice for a man to be healed, but the man was still healed.

Junia and Mason took note of every story, soon realizing that it would take an entire book just to document what had been done in this one night. It seemed it would take many libraries to document Sarx's work if this was what everyday with him was going to look like.

Hours later, the sun began to fade into the ocean and the most beautiful shades of pink, purple and orange were cast across the horizon, as though the sky itself were communicating some kind of blessing. That was when a family began to approach Sarx from behind. Mason had taken note of them thirty minutes earlier while chatting with the people in line. They looked like they could be trouble as their expressions seemed to display disgust.

"I think we've got a problem," Mason told Junia as the family left the solid streets and began to sink their feet into the sand.

Junia excused herself from her conversation with a young woman and joined Mason. "What is it?"

"That family over there," he pointed. "The ones walking up to Sarx. They've been eyeballing him for the last half hour or so and they don't look interested in getting in line."

Junia took note. "They look a bit familiar don't they?" she asked.

Mason squinted, trying to see what his sister saw. "A little bit. But we're so far from home that there's no way we've ever met them before."

"Perhaps in a dream?" asked Junia.

Mason shot his sister a strange glance.

"What?" laughed Junia. "Nothing is outside of the bounds of possibilities after what we've been through in the last few days!"

Mason smirked as he laughed out his nose. "Fair enough," he said. "But whoever they are, they're headed straight for Sarx."

"What should we do then?" asked Junia.

"I don't know," replied Mason, growing more nervous with their every step. "I imagine we'll have to try to fend them off."

"You mean *you'll* have to fend them off," said Junia.

"What?" replied Mason.

"You think that big guy there is going to threatened by a little girl?" pointed Junia.

Mason sighed and then began walking nervously towards the family, noting that they showed no response to his approach. Mason straightened up in attempts to make himself look bigger, but still nothing. In fact, the family walked right past him like he wasn't even there.

"Uh, excuse me," Mason sheepishly called, now behind them.

One of the siblings turned around and shot him a look showing him he meant business. With a raised eyebrow and a deep voice, he said, "What do you want kid?"

"Oh, uh," stumbled Mason as he tried to puff himself up a bit bigger. He pointed towards the line and tried to lower his voice a bit more to match the man's. "I just wanted to let you know that the line starts back there. These people have been standing in line since this afternoon, so if you don't want to start a riot, you'll want to make sure you wait like everyone else.

"We're well acquainted with Sarx," responded the man. "But who are you?"

Mason hadn't expected that. "Well I," he started, but then noticed Junia in the background waving to get his attention. "I, uh," he mumbled while trying to figure out what his sister was communicating. She was pointing to her nose over and over again. *What?* Mason lipped to his sister, clearly distracted. Junia pointed to the family and then at Sarx and then at her nose again. Mason glanced at the family's face with a confused look, but then his eyes grew wide. They had a family nose–one that he had seen before. *That's why they look so familiar,* he thought.

"Are you Sarx's family?" asked Mason with a confused tone. Hadn't he just seen Sarx's home in Heaven? Wasn't he a son of God, not a son of man? Wasn't God his Father?

"Jim!" exclaimed a voice that had snuck up on him as he was piecing everything together. "Brother! How long has it been?"

"Long enough for you to establish a following it seems," Jim responded with an annoyed tone.

"Be kind," said one of his sisters as she slapped Jim on the arm.

"Kind?" responded Jim. "Look at him! A little man from a little town acting like he's someone–like he has something to offer the world. Sarx, have you lost your mind?"

Mason looked for words to interject in Sarx's defense, but everything he could have said remained as an inhale, never making its way out of his mouth.

"Word has already moved throughout the city, Sarx. The religious folk say you have a demon that has made you insane," said another family member.

"Come on now Joey," responded Sarx. "You know me. I'm your own flesh and blood. Do I look insane to you?"

"Well, you've always been a bit different, bud," said another brother.

"Oh, and I suppose you're completely normal, Psy?" Sarx responded. "Guys, have you not heard about what's been going on here today?"

"We have," answered Jim. "Like Joey said–they say you have a demon."

"And do you agree?" Sarx asked with shock in his voice.

"That you have a demon?" another brother responded.

"Yes, Judah, that I have a demon." Annoyance could be heard quite clearly in Sarx's voice at this point.

"Well, I mean–" started Judah.

"Careful how you finish that sentence brother," Sarx said cutting him off. "For blasphemy against the Spirit of Light is a sin that cannot be reconciled."

"I'm not sure what you mean," responded Judah.

"That's because he's gone crazy," said Jim grabbing Sarx's shoulder. "Come on, Sarx, let's go home. Mom and Dad and the rest of your sisters are waiting for you."

"I'm busy right now, Jim," replied Sarx as he pulled away from him. "But I will come home when I'm done taking care of all of these people who have been waiting in line all day." Sarx turned around to see the crowd staring awkwardly at him, trying to get a good read on the situation.

"After all," continued Sarx, "my true family consists of those who do the will of the Creator." He grabbed a man's shoulder. "You are forgiven brother. Be healed." Then he took a woman's hand. "Be made well, my sister." Then he touched an older woman's ear. "Deaf spirit, leave my mother now." Each person was healed instantly.

"Sarx!" barked Jim.

"When. *I am*. done," Sarx said slowly and sternly, turning to Jim with an intense, albeit, hurt look on his face. He then called Junia and Mason over.

"Yes, Master?" asked Mason.

"From this point on, we'll need to move through the line a bit quicker. Can you communicate that to everyone?" Sarx asked.

"Can do," replied Mason as he set out to pass along the message.

"For what it's worth, Sarx, I believe in you," Junia blushed. "I don't think you're crazy or have a demon."

A big smile came over Sarx's face as he touched Junia's cheek. "My sister," he said.

# CHAPTER 12
## SON OF MAN

The walk to Sarx's house was taking a lot longer than Junia and Mason would have liked after having been on their feet for half the day. Junia also couldn't help but take note of the fishy smell still upon them. True, they had washed some of it off in the ocean, but it was going to take some real scrubbing to rid themselves of it completely.

Over the course of the walk, Sarx and his two followers slowed down to create some distance between themselves and the rest of the family. Every once in awhile Jim would look over his shoulder at the three and then turn forward and shake his head annoyedly.

"So, I'm a little confused," said Mason, breaking the silence.

"What?" said Sarx. "The last few days haven't been completely normal to you?"

Mason chuckled from the back of his throat. "I'm not entirely sure exactly what 'normal' is anymore."

"Yeah, I've been known to have that effect on people," laughed Sarx. Then looking up at his family, he mumbled, "Well, at least some people."

Mason rolled his eyes at them and nodded. "I guess it's just that I thought you were like… I don't know–a supernatural being or something? I mean, you do miracles. You took us to Heaven. You even referred to yourself as the 'Son of God'–as though the Creator is your Father or something. And honestly, that makes a whole lot more sense to me than you having siblings and whatnot."

"It's true, *I am* the Son of God," replied Sarx.

"How does that work?" asked Mason. "Is it like the other legends? You became a human-like baby and this family found you and adopted you and now you've grown up in their house and they don't know who you really are?"

"What? No!" laughed Sarx. "My birth-mother is just up ahead! You'll meet her."

"Okay, so then the other legends," continued Mason. "A spiritual being and a human being–"

"*Absolutely not!*" Sarx interrupted harshly. "Do not submit your thinking of the one and only God to the same ideology as the fallen spirits. My Father is holy and righteous–perfect in every way."

"Forgive me, Master," Mason bowed his head. "I guess I just don't understand."

A soft smile came to Sarx's firm face as he took pity on Mason. "Child, long ago my Father created this world as his Spirit of Light soared above the chaotic waters of this planet. That same Spirit is now inside of you, turning you into a new creation—a new person. Other spiritual beings may need to commit forbidden actions to make an heir, but the source of Creation does not. He speaks and it comes to be. And so, if the Spirit of Light can soar over chaos and create a planet full of life, then of course he can speak a child into existence if he wants to. Creation is his specialty."

"I suppose that makes sense," said Mason in a thoughtful tone. "But then doesn't that make you human?"

"Yes. *I am* the Son of Man," Sarx said proudly.

"But also the Son of God?" asked Mason.

"Yes," replied Sarx. "I existed as a spiritual being before I was born here as a physical being. Granted, I tend to refer to myself as the 'Son of Man.' It's really my opponents who tend to fling around my identity as the 'Son of God.'"

"And since you're the Son of God, that's partially why you can do miracles?" interjected Junia.

"I understand your thought process there Junia, but not exactly," smiled Sarx.

Junia put her hand on her forehead as though the conversation had given her a headache—or perhaps it was to hide her embarrassment. "I'm so confused," she said.

"*I am* fully the Son of Man," laughed Sarx. "*I am* one hundred percent human. Born of another human being. What you see before you is flesh and blood."

"But flesh and blood can't do miracles like you do," said Junia.

"Correct," smiled Sarx. "But the Spirit of Light can. And He has been doing so for a long time! Remember Morales and Vox?"

The two nodded in agreement.

"The two of them did all kinds of crazy supernatural things when they were on the earth. Did you think that they were any less than human?"

"No, of course not," said Junia. "That would be blasphemy."

"Right," agreed Sarx. "What they did, along with many others before me, was work with the Spirit of Light to use his power."

"But you gave us the Spirit of Light and we can't do those things," said Mason.

"Says who?" said Sarx, surprised at what he was hearing. "Really you two, have some faith."

"To what? To heal people? To cast out demons?" asked Mason.

"Yes! Exactly!" Sarx said loudly, catching the attention of his siblings up ahead. He then lowered his voice. "Few people throughout history have been anointed with the Spirit like you have. That will not always be the case, for when I return to Heaven, I will ask the Creator to send the Spirit to all who follow me. But right now, you guys are capable of operating in a power few have had the privilege of operating in."

"So we can heal people too?" asked Junia. "Like you?"

"Sort of like me," replied Sarx. "The Spirit of Light has anointed me to carry power in a capacity that no one else ever has. But I will teach you and extend the Spirit's power to you in different ways as we continue on our journey. And

I kid you not, despite all the crazy things you have seen me do and *will* see me do, my followers will do even crazier things."

Mason and Junia's eyes lit up at the promise. Crazier things? They themselves had the capacity to do what Sarx was doing? Their lives were changing rapidly and their understanding of the world was shifting every time this man opened his mouth.

"Okay, so just to be clear then, you are one hundred percent the Son of God," asked Mason.

"Yes. While there have been many sons of God recorded throughout the ages, *I am thee* Son of God. The one true Son of God. The heir to the throne. The child of the Creator. The full imager of what a true Son of God is supposed to image. The one who looks like what a true spiritual being was designed to be. God's one and only unique Son," answered Sarx.

"But then you're also one hundred percent the Son of Man?" asked Junia.

"One hundred percent," he replied. "I've emptied myself of that which was available to me as the Son of God and have made myself fully in the likeness of humanity. But setting aside my power as the Son of God to be a human does not rob me of my identity or authority as the Son of God. I have simply set aside that which isn't human so that I may be *thee* Son of Man."

"*Thee* Son of Man?" asked Junia.

"*Thee* Son of Man," replied Sarx. "For just as there are other sons of God, but none of them are *thee* son of God, so there are many sons of men, but none of them are *thee* Son of Man. *I am* the true man–the perfect imager of the Creator in human form. When you see me, you've seen the Father. And as the perfect human, *I am* the heir to the throne. The child of the Creator. The one who looks like what a true human was designed to be."

"And the reason you have power then–" started Mason.

"Is because I have the Spirit of Light fully working through me. Correct," finished Sarx.

"Sarx!" yelled a woman from the distance as she ran towards them. "Oh, there you are sweetheart!"

Sarx opened his arms wide as the woman blazed past his siblings. "Mama!" he smiled.

# CHAPTER 13
## Breakfast

Mason and Junia awoke from their slumber with full bellies and clean skin from their baths the night before.

"Good morning friends!" said Sarx's mother as she threw clean clothes on their sleepy faces. "Get dressed! I'm sure Sarx will have marching orders for you soon enough."

"What?" said Junia groggily as she rubbed her eyes. "Where... where is he?"

"Oh, you know Sarx," she replied. "He's always out early talking with his Father."

Mason wiped the sleep from his eyes. "I didn't see his dad last night," he said.

"No silly," laughed Sarx's Mom. "His *'Father'* Father."

## BREAKFAST

The two stared blankly at her, as they tried to remember the confusing conversation they had with Sarx on the way to his house.

"You know?" said the woman. "He's praying? To God?"

They both let out an, "Oooh," as they fell back on their pillows.

"Maybe you need to keep sleeping," she chuckled as she left the room, closing the door behind her. "Breakfast is ready when you are," called her muffled voice through the door.

Silence filled the room as the sibling's heavy eyelids began to close, when all of the sudden the doors to the window flew open.

"Hey guys!" yelled Sarx, startling them out from under their blankets and into standing position, their hearts pounding. Sarx took a good look at the frazzled siblings. "I'm surprised Mama didn't wake you up already."

Junia let out a yawn as she tried to fix her crazy hair. "She did," she said. "We were just getting up."

"Uh huh," Sarx grinned. "Well get dressed. I imagine breakfast is ready and we'll want to eat before we leave in the next few hours."

"Are we heading back to the beach?" asked Mason, picking up his new clothes.

"Nope," replied Sarx.

"Why not?" asked Mason. "There's probably a whole crowd lined up waiting to see if you'll come back."

"No doubt," said Sarx. "But that's not where my Father wants us today. So up and at 'em!"

Junia headed to the bathroom to get dressed and then the two met up with the family for breakfast. The conversation was less than delightful, to say the least. Sarx's family was still chastising him for the events of the night before.

It hurt Junia's heart to hear the way they talked about him. Clearly they didn't understand who their own sibling was—they just thought he was mad. *Perhaps that's the way people always come across when they're imaging God,* she thought. She eventually had enough of the conversation and tuned out until Sarx's mother's voice brought her back.

"Sarx, do you remember when you were a young boy and we went into town for the holidays?" she smiled.

"Aw, Ma, not this story again," Jim rolled his eyes.

"He had your Father and I terrified!" she laughed. "Really though, I don't know why I even share the story—it's quite embarrassing. We were half way home when we realized Sarx wasn't anywhere to be found!"

"What?" smiled Junia. "What did you do?"

"Well, we tried to remember the last time we had seen him but—oh, I was completely useless—a nervous wreck if ever there was one. How had I left my baby behind on the holidays? I get goosebumps just thinking about it!"

"That's why I'm always surprised you share this story," said one of Sarx's sisters.

"Yes, well, it's because of the point the story serves," said the mother with a smile. "By the time we finally got back to town I thought he was gone for sure. It had been three days! No child could remain still that long. Where did he sleep? Who did he stay with? Surely he had gone to find us and had gotten lost!"

"But?" asked Mason.

"But we got to town and there he was. Sitting amongst the religious teachers of the city and listening to them and asking them questions. Three days! Three days had gone by and he looked like he hadn't even noticed! He was too busy learning about God." A smile overtook her face as she sat back and took a bite of an apple. "I remember thinking to myself, *Who is this? What kind of boy spends time studying when he could be outside playing?*"

Then she pointed to her sons with a stern look on her face. "That crowd yesterday was not the first he's entertained. You should have seen it. Everyone was amazed at his knowledge–that a child could think on the level of these adults. Who would have ever expected such a thing? A son of a craftsman, behaving like a scribe without any of the proper background to be one."

"Mom, all memories tend to change with age," said Judah.

The mother's face took on a bit of a crazed look as she threw her apple core right by Judah's face and into the trash can behind him. Judah's eyes grew big as his mother bit her lip with a smile. Then she looked deep into Sarx's eyes.

"You know, when I was in my teens I thought I might be a singer. I wanted to write songs and share them with the world," she said

"What happened, Mom?" asked one of her daughters. "You have such a pretty voice. You could have done it."

"Thanks sweetie," she smiled. "I stopped trying because along the way I learned a lesson. In order to get your start, you often need the people around you to support you–to see your music the way you see it."

"Nobody supported you?" asked Junia, fearing she was entering a conversation that was not hers to be had. But the mother looked at her with bright eyes.

"Afraid not dear," she said. "To them I was just Maria–the next door neighbor. Daughter of a farmer–and a *daughter* at that. I was the girl they had watched grow up. The baby whose diapers they changed. People didn't hate my music or anything, but they certainly thought my dream was ridiculous. Because again, I was just… me. Just Maria."

"What's your point Mom?" asked Joey.

"My point," started Maria with an intensity in her voice, "is that a prophet is not accepted in his hometown–not even, it seems, by his own family. Sarx hasn't done anything wrong to be treated the way you're all treating him. The fault lies on you and, quite frankly, your inability to see God at work in your brother's life."

Maria's whole family looked down at the table and hid their eyes as they debated if their mother's point was valid or not. Was their brother really a prophet? They only had a brief second to process the idea when there was a knock on the front door.

Maria looked out the window and then turned to Sarx. "Speaking of your hometown," she said.

# CHAPTER 14
## THE CROWD

"Hey Maria," said the man at the door. "Word has gotten around this morning that your son is home."

"Okay?" answered Maria. "What's this about Robert? I can't imagine you all just wanted to stop by and say hello?"

"Uh, no, not exactly," he responded. "Look: Word on the street is that Sarx has been getting quite a bit of attention in the city as a teacher of sorts or something like that."

"And?" Maria furrowed her brow.

"And, well… I guess we just wanted to make sure you had him under control is all," Robert explained.

## THE CROWD

"I see. Let me just check on that really quick," she said turning her head inside and calling into the dining room. "Sarx, there's a crowd out here that wants to make sure I have my adult son under control. Are you all good dear?"

Sarx smirked at his siblings, wiped his mouth with a napkin and joined Maria at the door. "Hey neighbors. What can I do for you?"

The crowd suddenly felt a mix of emotions. Most could pinpoint it as discomfort, but the source of that discomfort was confusing. Some could note that their discomfort stemmed from being in the presence of a man whom so many miracles had been attributed to the night before, but others found their discomfort to be born primarily out of disgust for this nobody who suddenly was a somebody. Robert felt more disgust.

"Oh, hey Sarx," Robert said as he cleared his throat. "We just wanted to check in on your family and see how they were doing. We had heard some stories recently that might draw attention to them."

"Miracles you mean?" grinned Sarx.

An annoyed grin took over Robert's expression. "Sure, son. Stories of *so-called* miracles."

"So-called?" Sarx was taken aback. "One minute a boy is blind and the next he sees. How is that *so-called*?"

Suddenly there was tangible amount of anger in Robert's voice. "It's *so-called*, because it's attributed to you, boy. You're a woodworker! From a family of woodworkers! Not a priest or a prophet. Seems you've overstepped your bounds. You should be listening to the men of God, not acting like a man of God yourself!"

"Yeah!" echoed some of the other neighbors in the mob.

Sarx shook his head up and down as though he understood their concern, though it was clear from his facial expression that he didn't agree at all. "I have met many of your *so-called* men of God, Robert. And I must say, if those are the men you consider the best examples of God, then I fear you know very little about who God actually is."

"You better watch your mouth," Robert said harshly. "You walk around all high and mighty, but you're nothing special. You don't have powers! You perform– *I don't know*–parlor tricks. Or perhaps you're leading people into some kind of psychological madness. Or maybe you're using some of the Plaintiff's magic–but you are certainly not–"

"Careful friend," said Sarx as his stern voice cut through the crowd.

"Excuse me?" asked Robert.

"All things can be excused," said Sarx. "But blasphemy of the Spirit of Light is the one sin that will be reckoned against humanity for all eternity."

"I did no such thing!" exclaimed Robert.

"No, but you did," responded Sarx. "My miracles are the work of the Spirit of Light, himself. And you, in your ignorance just attributed the Spirit's work to the Plaintiff's work and have blasphemed him. Do you think the Spirit of Love wants anything to do with the work of hatred? Watch your tongue before you condemn yourself."

"You lecture me, boy?" asked Robert.

"And more," said Sarx. "For as you've heard, I'm not only full of lessons, but healing. And there is freedom from your oppression today if any of you come to me."

# THE CROWD

Sarx held out his arms, waiting for someone to step forward. But the moment grew awkward as no one answered the invitation. Robert crossed his arms and grinned.

"No one needs healing today?" asked Sarx. "Not even you, Cindy? After all those migraines over the years? You have one right now, do you not?"

The woman drew back in the crowd and gazed down at her sandals, pretending everyone's attention wasn't focused on her. But then the migraine pounded in the front of her head and she reached up and grabbed it, as though her brain was going to burst through her skull. She gasped as a tear rolled down her face. Then, without looking up to see the disapproval of those around her, she walked quickly up to Sarx while holding her head in her hands.

Sarx slowly removed her hands from her forehead and looked into her eyes. "There's no need to be embarrassed," he said. "For you have asked for the kingdom to come upon you today." He placed three fingers on her temples and whispered, "Be gone," instantly relieving the pressure from her head.

Cindy felt clearer than she had ever felt. She collapsed into Sarx's chest, sobbing tears of joy. "Praise God!" she exclaimed between gasps for air. "I've been healed! It's gone!"

Maria stepped in and pulled Cindy off of Sarx's chest and onto her shoulder. She rubbed the back of her head and whispered, "Amen, amen, amen," as her eyes swelled with her own tears.

Sarx briefly looked back into the house to see his brothers and sisters gazing at him in wonder. Sarx nodded at Mason and Junia and then turned back to the crowd to see expressions of surprise. But then Robert shook his head as though to flick the expression off his face. The wonder left his eyes and disgust filled him once again. He turned back to the crowd and yelled out, "Parlor tricks!"

"God promised your ancestors that he would set up a kingdom," said Sarx with fire in his eyes. "Will you not accept the signs of that kingdom being performed right in front of you?"

"*We will not*," said Robert through gritted teeth.

A look of deep pain entered Sarx's face. Then the fire returned. "Then the kingdom will be handed over to those who see, believe and respond and you will not take part in it. Just as you wipe your feet off after being around those you consider unclean, so will I wipe my feet after being around you."

"Who utters blasphemy now?" yelled Robert, the crowd cheering in return. "Will you be the town responsible for giving birth to this heretic?"

"No!" they shouted.

"Then take him to the cliff and end his life!" Robert yelled.

"Yeah!" the crowd agreed.

Sarx put his hand on his mother's shoulder. "Like you said," he smiled. "A prophet is not accepted in his hometown."

Maria smiled as Mason and Junia ran to Sarx's side. "Be good, Son."

"Can I behave any other way?" he winked.

He grabbed Mason and Junia's hands and began to walk forward into the crowd. The siblings braced for impact, but it seemed as though everyone was

## THE CROWD

walking right around them. In a matter of seconds they were at the back of the crowd and on their way out of the town.

"Where is he?" they heard voices shouting. "He was just here a second ago!"

"What just happened?" Mason whispered to Junia.

"I've learned to stop asking questions," Junia answered, her smile hiding her pounding heart.

# CHAPTER 15
## Directions

"We've been walking for some time," Junia said, interrupting the sounds of nature that had filled their otherwise silent journey. "Is there somewhere in particular that we're headed?"

"Well of course we're headed somewhere in particular," laughed Sarx. "Did you think we were just wandering around aimlessly?"

"No, not exactly," blushed Junia. "I guess I just find your actions... mysterious."

"Mysterious?" questioned Sarx.

"Yeah. It's like–*how do I say this*... It's like everything you do has purpose. Like every step counts or is guided along by providence or something," Junia explained.

# DIRECTIONS

"And that's mysterious?" asked Sarx.

"Well yeah," Junia answered. "My life doesn't look like that. If anything I feel like I'm always in the wrong place at the wrong time doing the wrong thing. But you–you're basically the opposite."

"Hmm," Sarx pondered aloud. "Seems to me your definition of mysterious matches my definition of normal."

"How's that?" Mason chimed in.

"Long ago, humanity lived in the very presence of the Creator–a garden in the most sacred of sacred spaces on the planet. His presence was so close and so tangible that you could hear his footsteps shifting through the lush grass. The earliest humans carried on conversations with him just as casually as we're talking now. There was no hindrance in the relationship–just God and humanity at play, teaming up together to rule the planet." Sarx wiped the sweat from his brow as he continued to walk in the hot sun. "So what you just described as mysterious is really about as normal as life could have been. But with the current corruption in the way, that kind of life isn't as simple as it used to be."

"I wish we could get back to that," said Mason longingly.

"In due time, brother. In due time," acknowledged Sarx. "But for now you have me to guide you. The providence you spoke of, Junia, is simply my will being completely conformed to my Father's. The Spirit of Light leads me every step of the way, showing me what my Father is doing. He and I are so intertwined that, really, I can only do what he does."

"Wow," Junia marveled. "I wish I could see what the Creator is doing with the same kind of detail as you."

"Well you're in luck then," smiled Sarx. "Because when you've seen me, you've seen the Father. Therefore, you two are being given a glimpse of God that most could only hope for."

"Okay," Junia grinned, her face lighting up in a way that was impossible not to notice. "So then where is the Spirit taking us now?"

Sarx stopped and turned to look at the siblings. "Close your eyes for a moment," he instructed them, followed by a long pause. "What do you hear?"

The children closed their eyes and remained quiet for some time. Well, really it was only about twenty seconds, but it felt like twenty minutes. The two soaked in the sounds around them and began to speak them out once the silence had become too uncomfortable.

"Birds," said Mason.

"The wind in the trees," said Junia.

"My pulse," said Mason.

"My breath," said Junia.

"Yes, very good," said Sarx. "But I'm not talking about your natural ears. What do you hear with your spiritual ears?" His question was met with an even longer pause.

"Uh…" laughed Mason. "Yeah, I got nothing."

"I'm not sure I know how to use those," said Junia.

# DIRECTIONS

"Nonsense!" said Sarx. "Just as your own spirit lives inside of you, so does the Creator's Spirit live inside of you—for you are a new creation! You mean to tell me that you can't hear him even a little bit?"

"Like I said—that kind of thing is mysterious," explained Junia, her eyes still closed.

"With enough practice, you may find it to be much more normal than you think," said Sarx. "Look, you can hear your own spirit, right?"

"I guess," said Junia.

"Yes, of course you can. Your spirit searches the depths of your heart and knows all that is going on inside of you. That's why when life gets out of control you sometimes scream out, 'I can't even hear myself think!' You feel a disconnect—like you can't get in touch with yourself. Surely you've had that happen before?" asked Sarx.

"Well sure, everyone has I imagine," replied Junia.

"Right. So what do you do in that moment to get in touch with yourself again?" asked Sarx. "Play music? Lie on your bed? Take a bath? Sit in silence?"

"I guess I like to take a walk through nature and clear my head," she answered.

"Perfect," said Sarx. "Now if that's what you need to do to get in touch with your own spirit, which searches the depths of your thoughts, then do that to listen to God's Spirit, which searches the depths of his thoughts. Of course, the Spirit of Light is often much quieter than your own spirit, so you'll need to really practice being quiet to discern what is your spirit and what is God's spirit."

"Okay," said Junia, closing her eyes even more tightly.

"Junia," laughed Sarx. "Stop trying so hard. Don't work it up. Open your eyes."

Junia opened her eyes and was instantly reminded that they had been walking through a forest for the last few miles, which meant that her chance to walk through nature in attempts to listen to God was available to her right then.

"Walk up ahead of us," instructed Sarx. "Try to listen to the Spirit as you do. Remember, he's already inside of you. Just quiet yourself enough to discern his Spirit from yours. We'll walk behind you. When you think he's maybe told you something, let me know what you think he said."

Junia boldly walked ahead of the other two, though she feared that she would fail this little exercise. Sarx seemed to hear so naturally, so easily, so normally—and she did not. But she was willing to try. She took a deep breath as Sarx's words returned to her mind: *Stop trying so hard. Don't work it up*. And soon, she had quieted her thoughts. Within a few minutes she felt she might have heard something.

"The Southern Mountains?" she said. "Is that where we're going?"

"Aha!" exclaimed Sarx. "See, I told you you could do it!"

Junia blushed. "I don't know. It all feels a little phony. After I finally calmed down I realized where the sun was and that we were walking south. Then I think I just concluded that we were headed to the Southern Mountains because you were talking about the Dragon of the South earlier."

"So you think it was by pure logic that you deduced that we were walking into the most unthinkable place we could go?" asked Sarx with a grin.

## DIRECTIONS

"Well, when you put it that way," chuckled Junia.

"That's the thing with the Spirit of Light," said Sarx. "A lot of people think that if he were to speak to them, he would be booming in their ears with audible words. But that's not often his way. And even when he does speak with volume, some still confuse his words for thunder. To walk in step with him, you must practice listening. You must create a playground for your spirit and his Spirit to mingle. And when you do that, it will sometimes be hard to decide where your direction came from. Was it him? Or was it you?"

"I hate to interrupt," said Mason from behind the two. "But are we really headed towards the Dragon's Lair? To the Plaintiff himself?"

"Indeed," answered Sarx.

"Okay then," said Mason, clearing his throat to make way for some heavy sarcasm. "I just like to make sure I'm prepared ahead of time to meet a fire-breathing dragon on his turf, which, by the way, is well known to be where the realm of the dead is located. You know—no big deal or anything."

"Well now you'll be prepared!" grinned Sarx. "Though we do have a few places we need to stop by first on our way there."

"Somehow I knew you were going to say that," said Junia.

"See?" said Sarx. "You're getting ahold of how he speaks!"

"What?" asked Junia. "Oh... I see. Interesting."

"Indeed. And now I believe it's time for you guys to experience the Spirit's power a bit more tangibly," said Sarx.

"How do you mean?" asked Mason.

"I mean it's time you two start doing the things I do," he responded. "I mentioned on the way home that eventually the time would come where you two would also need to perform miracles. Now is that time."

"Okay then," said Mason, trying to hold back a smile. The idea of walking around with such powers was quite alluring to him, but he didn't want others to catch onto it.

"Don't act like you're not excited Mason," smiled Sarx.

Mason tensed up as Sarx discerned his emotions so easily. It was almost as though he knew exactly what he was thinking. *Was that the Spirit, too?* he wondered.

"It would do you good to acknowledge that pride," said Sarx. "Pride was the Plaintiff's downfall and humans have fallen prey to its effects since the beginning. Those who follow me must walk humbly and peaceably. Godly power must be practiced in step with the Spirit."

"I imagine there's no other way to use that power," returned Mason.

"Don't be so sure," said Sarx with a warning in his eyes. "But you two have seen me work with the Spirit, so now I'm sending you out to imitate me. Go and cast out demons, heal whatever sickness comes your way–raise the dead if you have to! The Spirit will empower you to do such things, so place your faith in him and not yourselves."

Now Mason had a full smile across his face. He couldn't help it. But once he noticed his expression, he acknowledged his pride as Sarx had warned him. He then cleared his throat and said, "And where do we do this at?"

## DIRECTIONS

"Right here," said Sarx, moving a large leaf out of his face and revealing a village at the edge of the forest. "These people know me. Or at least they should."

"Did you used to live here or something?" asked Junia.

"No," replied Sarx. "But I am the person they've been waiting for God to send to them. So show them the works of the kingdom as the Spirit enables you to perform them and then tell them about me and what I'm doing. If they accept you, then they accept me and the peace I bring. If they reject you, don't take it to heart; for they're really rejecting me."

Sarx put his hands on their backs and pushed them out of the forest and into the open. "Meet me by the waterfall on the other side of town at dusk!" he yelled as he walked back into the forest, his voice growing more and more distant as he walked away. "Oh, and some are going to want to pay you for what the Spirit does through you. But you're not here to make a profit so refuse their money. But do feel free to share a meal with them if they offer. Go in faith. You don't need a staff or bread or bag or sword or extra clothes or anything of the sort to get you through this work. Trust in God to provide!"

Junia and Mason looked towards each other. Then towards the village. Then back at each other.

"Well," said Junia. "Here we go."

# CHAPTER 16
## THE DEMONIC ARMY

"Ah, there you guys are!" smiled Sarx as Mason and Junia ran up to meet him by the waterfall. Its waters gushed over the steep cliff there at the edge of town.

"We did it!" exclaimed Mason. "We saw a skin disease fall right off a person!"

"And I told a demon to go and it did!" smiled Junia, her face beaming. Clearly it had been liberating to go from being mastered by a demon to mastering a demon.

Mason then paused for a moment and recognized that Sarx was joined by ten others who looked to be about Mason's age. At first he had thought they were just a random crowd, but now he was fairly certain Sarx had brought them here.

"Are these friends of yours?" asked Mason, breathing heavily from the excitement of sharing he and Junia's stories from the day.

"Ah, yes. Mason, Junia, I'd like you to meet the gang!" exclaimed Sarx. He then began to point down the line. "This is Jimmy and Johnny–they're brothers. Also, meet Phil, Bart, Tom, Matt, Jim, Thad, Sim, and Judah."

"That's going to be a lot to remember," laughed Mason with wide eyes.

"Indeed," nodded Sarx. "Though with all the people you've met recently, if you just try calling people 'Jim' or 'Judah,' you're bound to be right a fair amount of the time."

Mason and Junia laughed and then shook hands and exchanged pleasantries with the men as Sarx cooked some fish over a campfire. Within time they all joined Sarx and began to eat dinner together. They took turns telling funny stories, each one of them trying to one-up the last, which created a night full of laughter. Bart laughed so hysterically at one point that he fell backwards off the log he was sitting on and didn't stop laughing for five minutes. Sarx got quite a kick out of this and let out a long belly laugh. Eventually Bart pulled himself back up to his seat and wiped the tears from his eyes. He let out a high pitched sigh and rubbed his cheeks as though they were in pain.

Suddenly, a very cold breeze blew across the group and Sarx's expression turned from joy to something like annoyance. The whole group grew quiet as a few of them shivered and rubbed their arms. A rancid smell came with the wind that caused them to gag and cover their noses. Many of them noted a figure approaching Sarx from behind and they squinted to get a better look. As it grew closer the men gasped and many stood up to protect themselves. Mason instinctively pulled Junia up to her feet and then shielded her with his body.

Sarx was the only one still sitting, and he did so expressionlessly while turning a stick in the campfire.

"Uh, Sarx," gulped Thad. "There's a–"

"Yes, Thad, I know," replied Sarx. He pushed his stick into the ground to pull himself up and then turned to face the being. "There's a zombie behind me."

It was the most unusual, most terrifying zombie anyone had ever seen. He wore little more than a loin cloth, displaying much of his large muscular body for all to see. He had chains around his wrists and ankles as though someone had tried to attach him to a wall, but he had just ripped the chains in half. There were gashes all across his arms, his chest, his legs and his back as though he had been trying to cut his very skin off. His flesh was quite rotted in some places, exposing the muscles underneath. The bags under his eyes drooped so low that one feared his eyeballs might fall right out.

But there was something about those eyes. They looked tired and beat. It was as though no one could be more disgusted with the zombie than himself.

"Sarx, we need to get out of here!" exclaimed Judah.

"There is no need to be afraid," said Sarx.

"But he'll kill us!" yelled Judah.

"Have some faith, Judah," Sarx continued without raising his voice. "Take strength in the fact that I know the full weight of what's in front of us and yet I am not afraid."

"Uh, I'm pretty sure we all see the full weight of this situation," said Judah as he accepted that their group was not leaving and took on a defensive posture.

"Do you?" asked Sarx as he turned back to look at Judah. He then snapped his finger so loud that the sound reverberated throughout the forest, even overtaking the roar of the waterfall.

Judah's eyes grew wide and his defensive posture immediately fell along with everyone else's. Their eyes had been opened to see something they hadn't seen before: A horde of about two thousand demons stood in front of them in all kinds of shapes and sizes. Big ones and small ones; some with nasty teeth and others that looked like reptiles. All matters of sin could be seen in their eyes. You could feel temptation just by looking at them.

The fight was unfair. Before their eyes had been opened, Sarx's friends had thought that *maybe* the twelve of them could take on this muscular zombie, but now that they had seen this army of darkness in front of them, they shrunk back to hide behind some trees. Now it was just one versus two thousand. The twelve tried to persuade Sarx to run, but he continued to stand his ground as the army approached him at a zombie-like pace.

A demon reached into the zombie's heart and twisted it, causing the zombie to let out an impossibly loud roar. But Sarx stood still.

Six steps until they had met and overwhelmed Sarx completely. Beads of sweat dripped off Mason's forehead.

Five steps. Four steps. Three steps. Junia imagined what her hero would look like after a zombie bite and her heart sank into her stomach.

Two steps. One step.

Time was up.

The zombie stood a full foot above Sarx and looked down at him with eyes of sadness while Sarx stared at him with eyes of compassion. And there they stood, just staring at each other for what felt like half an hour, but was probably only a minute or two. Sarx's friends watched from the trees in amazement. It almost looked as though Sarx and the zombie were having a silent conversation with one another.

The cold wind suddenly stopped and Sarx moved for the first time in the battle. It wasn't much–all he did was turn his gaze from the zombified man in front of him to the demons on the left of him. In doing so, the demons immediately fell to their knees in complete and total fear. And as Sarx moved his gaze to the right of the zombie, each and every demon–*including the zombie himself*–fell to the ground and bowed before Sarx.

The demon that had reached into the zombie's heart tried to lift up his eyes just enough to see Sarx's chin. He then clasped his hands together and said, "Please Son of God! Please don't torture us!"

"Like you have tortured this man?" asked Sarx.

"Please… Please, swear to God that you won't torture us!" said the demon, completely ignoring Sarx's comment. "If you must remove us from this man, then so be it, but please–*please* don't send us out of the country!"

"Yes, that would be most unpleasant for you, wouldn't it?" asked Sarx.

"Yes, Son of God, very much so! Very unpleasant!" replied the demon as his troop quivered behind him.

"As unpleasant as what you've done to this man?" asked Sarx.

The demon grunted bitterly, still afraid to look into Sarx's eyes. Without lifting his head, he looked left and right, as though to look for an idea. Then it seemed that one popped into his mind.

"How about this, Master: There is a large farm on the other side of this waterfall. We won't afflict this man anymore, but instead we'll dwell in the animals there! No more humans will be hurt and we get to stay in the country. It's a win-win!" persuaded the demon.

Sarx chuckled. "You think that's a win-win?"

"Yes, Master," replied the demon.

A smirk grew on Sarx's face which caused the demon to shiver. "Then have it your way, spirit," he said.

Desperate to get away from Sarx as soon as possible, the lead demon yelled out, "Follow me, soldiers!" The two thousand quickly took to the air and flew over the waterfall towards the farm as the zombie fell on his side. As each demon flew away, his body began to look more and more human. Sarx's team watched in amazement as color returned to his skin and his flesh began to heal. As the last one flew away, he became completely and totally human again. All that remained were scars from the wounds he had scratched into himself.

"One of you give him your cloak," Sarx said, turning to his friends.

Phil stumbled over a few sticks as he left the trees, pulling off his cloak along the way and laying it over the former-zombie's passed out body. The rest of the crew made their way out behind him.

"I ain't never buying meat from that farm again," said Bart in attempts to ease his nerves with humor.

Sarx grinned at the comment. "I don't think you'll need to worry about that," he said.

"Why not?" asked Tom.

"Do you recall how God's people removed sin from the community in the past?" Sarx asked.

"Sure," Tom replied. "The community was to confess their sin into an animal and then that animal was sent out into the desert where the demon Azazel dwelt—for sin belongs with Azazel and not with God's community."

"You mean we *used to* send animals into the desert," Matt interjected. "But then we got afraid that they'd come back to us with all of our sin, so we just started pushing them off cliffs to make sure they couldn't come back."

"It's actually a pretty common technique among exorcists today to try to move demons into animals," Tom added, causing everyone to look at him curiously. "At least from what I've seen. Granted, a lot of times the animal is killed or drowned after the transference to ensure that the demon isn't still around. But even though Sarx only did half of that ceremony, it was still certainly the most incredible exorcism that's ever been done."

"That's ever been done, *so far*," Sarx emphasized as he knelt over the zombie's body.

Suddenly there was a loud rumble coming from the other side of the waterfall that shook the earth beneath their feet.

"What is that?" asked Jimmy.

"*That*," paused Sarx, "would be the other half the exorcism."

Suddenly, a barrage of farm animals burst out of the forest on the other side of the waterfall, running madly towards the wide rushing river. There were so many farm animals that many of Sarx's friends moved back in fear that they were about to be caught up in the stampede, even though they knew that their fear was unreasonable given how wide the river was.

Or was it unreasonable? So many animals were falling into the river at one time that other animals were getting just enough time to walk on their backs. This continued to happen until nearly all two thousand animals had piled into the river, most of them falling over the waterfall's edge to their death.

Just when they thought the stampede was over, a rabid bull came flying out of the forest at full speed with his head hung low to gore whatever he found in front of him. He made his way across the shifting bridge of animal backs and leapt high through the air at Sarx.

But Sarx had no fear. In fact, he walked towards the bull as though to encourage him to try and touch him. The bull was midair at full speed and one foot from colliding with Sarx when a huge wave came out of nowhere and barreled the ox and all the other animals over the waterfall's edge.

As soon as all the animals had plummeted to their deaths, the river became more calm than it had been the entire evening—the waterfall a trickle in comparison to the roar it had been before. Sarx's followers stood there in silence, gazing at this man—*or whatever he was*—standing on the edge of the quiet river.

Johnny, with both awe and fear in his voice, leaned over to Junia and whispered, "Demons listen to him. The waves listen to him. Who exactly is this guy?"

A slow grin grew on Junia's face. "You have no idea," she said slowly.

"They're in Levi's domain now," said Sarx as he closed his eyes and took in a slow deep breath. It looked as though he was breathing in an atmosphere that wasn't there before. Mason couldn't help but acknowledge that something did feel different—as though a pressure or weight he hadn't realized he'd been carrying since he arrived in the village had been lifted off his shoulders. Things felt cleaner. Brighter. More spacious.

But then this moment of peace was interrupted by a furious growl that sounded like it was miles away. As though something far from them had just suffered from the great work done in this place. The team looked around, trying to trace where it was coming from, but then their attention was drawn back by a quiet groan. They turned to see Sarx helping the former zombie up to his feet. Mason jumped in to help pull him up. The two of them walked him over to a log to sit on.

"Thank you," the man groaned as he grabbed his forehead to ease a headache. His shoulders then began to shake as he wept before them. *"Thank you so much,"* he cried.

"Welcome back to the land of the living," said Sarx as the man wiped his nose and wrapped his cloak tightly around him after noticing Junia. "What's your name?"

The man's weeping turned slowly to confused laughter. "I... I don't remember," he said.

"Jim is a pretty safe bet," chuckled Bart.

Sarx laughed and shrugged. "He's not wrong. But either way, you don't need to know your previous name. For now on you will be known as Sophroneo."

"Thank you, sir," said the large man as he stood up and put his fist to his chest and bowed his head. "I will take any name you give me. Please allow me to join your team and serve you."

Sarx smiled and patted the man on the shoulder. "You would be very helpful on our journey my friend," he said. "But you can do more good here in your homeland than you can do on the road with me. Go and show everyone here what God has done for you so that they might be in awe and wonder. Having known you before, no one here will be able to look at you now and not believe in me."

"Yes sir," replied Sophroneo. "Though, if I may, I'd still much rather go with you. This town is understandably not all that fond of me and I really think I could be of help on your journey. I could be your bodyguard or something."

Sarx let out a small chuckle. "I admire your passion Sophroneo. But there is no need to guard a body when its purpose is to be destroyed."

"I don't understand," said Sophroneo.

"I fear that my friends do not either," Sarx explained as he turned to them. "But you will all see within time that to follow me is to be *all in* for my Father. For he who made your body may require it to do his work."

"Yes, Sarx," Mason spoke up. "I give my very life to this cause."

"That is wonderful enthusiasm Mason," acknowledged Sarx. "But I fear that in your passion you misunderstand what I mean. For the Kingdom of God fights with tactics you do not yet understand."

Mason nodded with a bit of embarrassment on his face as Sarx put his hands on Sophroneo's shoulders. "You are free my friend," he said. "Free to live. Free to love. Free to follow me. Return home and show your community how the kingdom of Heaven has come upon you. And beware future demonic attacks. Despite how crammed for space they were, those demons found a home in you and they will try to move back in. On top of that, they'll bring more of their friends in an effort to get back in. But I have empowered you to break the cycle of corruption and sin and the attack of any demon. Keep your eyes focused on God and he will show you the way."

"Thank you sir," said Sophroneo, once again putting his hand to his chest and bowing his head.

Sarx nodded silently with a smile and then turned to the twelve. "Time to go friends. You can't remove two thousand farm animals in a night and not upset the community. They'll expect us to be on our way, so let's grab our things."

The group picked up their backpacks and put on their coats and made their way south into the forest. And as Sarx entered the forest he turned one last time to his new friend.

"Stay sane, Sophroneo," he winked.

"Yes sir," Sophroneo waved.

# CHAPTER 17
## LIFE AND DEATH AND AFTER

"So let me see if I have this straight," Tom said to Sarx as Mason rolled his eyes. "We're just going to walk right up to the Plaintiff's doorstep–to the dragon's very lair–and hope that everything goes okay?"

"I'm sorry, Tom," chimed in Thad. "Did you not see what Sarx just did to an army of demons?"

"Oh, I'm sorry, Thad," replied Tom sarcastically. "I guess I just have an irrational fear of dragons or something–especially when they hold the power of death and when they make the very gates of Hell their home!"

"Wait," paused Junia. "The Plaintiff lives in Hell?"

"He rules over the dead!" interjected Bart. "Where else should he live, but where the dead go!"

# LIFE AND DEATH AND AFTER

"Well, not all of the dead," said Mason.

"What's that?" asked Bart.

"Not all of the dead," repeated Mason. "The dead who followed God in life join his kingdom."

"That's fanciful thinking," said Bart. "Pleasant thinking for sure, but fanciful. Some of the priests aren't even sure there is an afterlife."

"Then why do you fear the gates of Hell?" asked Sarx.

"Well, I mean… it's Hell, ya know?" replied Bart. "If it wasn't to be feared then it'd be called… Happy Land or something."

"Life does not end in the grave, brother," said Sarx.

"It's true! We've seen the saints of old!" said Mason excitedly.

Bart let out a boisterous laugh. "What's this then?" he said. "You see dead people, do you?"

"Save it for later, Mason. They're not yet ready," warned Sarx. "Bart, you said yourself that the Plaintiff is the ruler of the dead."

"I did," said Bart. "What of it?"

"Well, if my Father is the opposite of the Plaintiff, what would that make his title?" asked Sarx.

Bart paused for a moment. "Ruler of the living I suppose?" he answered.

"And tell me, of which of those two kingdoms did our zombie friend belong? The kingdom of the dead or the kingdom of the living?" asked Sarx.

"At first? The kingdom of the dead I guess," answered Bart. "The man was a hollow shell of a human. He had the smell of death all over him."

"You say, 'at first.' Does that mean you would now qualify him differently?" asked Sarx.

"Well sure, he's alive now and doing the Creator's work," said Bart.

"So then he has given his allegiance to God's kingdom of the living, rather than to the Plaintiff's kingdom of the dead," Sarx pointed out.

"Well, sure," said Bart.

"So when his mortal body dies and his spirit moves into the afterlife, whose kingdom will he join?" asked Sarx. "The kingdom of life or the kingdom of death?"

"The kingdom of life, I suppose?" said Bart. "But I'm confused. Are not all spirits by definition, dead?"

"Perhaps in the way *you* think of death," said Sarx. "But to be alive or dead is about more than having a body that breathes air. There are many zombies out there who have just enough makeup to hide their decay. In fact, some of the dead have such expensive makeup that they are the most beautiful people you'll ever see. But don't be fooled, they're walking caskets without my Father."

"I'm not sure I fully understand," said Bart. "I mean, we still all die in the way that we think of death, don't we? That is, all of our bodies turn to rot and whatnot."

"Sure," said Sarx. "But my Father has a plan for me to put an end to that kind of death too."

"Okay then," said Bart as he stopped to think through everything he was just taught. "You know, I don't think I understand anything we just said." Everyone laughed.

"I know I certainly didn't understand anything you said," replied Sarx. Everyone laughed harder.

"Alright, so then what's the mark of a person of life?" asked Matt. "I mean, obviously there's the loving and following God thing, but I feel like there's a lot of people who claim they do that and they look like nothing more than dragons."

"Only God can judge between saints and dragons," replied Sarx. "But you'll recognize the citizens of Heaven by their truth and citizens of Hell by their lies. The people of light by their ability to hear God speak and the people of darkness by their inability. The followers of the Son of God by their care for the poor and the followers of the sons of God by their oppression. Simply put, you'll recognize the saints by their good fruit and dragons by their bad fruit. Love—*actual love, which is defined as the Creator himself*—is the mark of a person of life. Hate—*though called love by some*—is the mark of a person of death."

"Wow," said Matt. "There's a lot there to discern between."

"And that final discernment is God's to make—*not yours*—so be cautious of your pride, lest you bring judgment upon yourself," warned Sarx. "You must use your discernment to learn how to grow those around you from where they are currently, to where they need to be. From death to life. From darkness to light. Or perhaps even from a dim light to a brighter one. You must all grow from the glories that are available to you on the earth now, to the greater glories that will be available to you beyond the afterlife."

"Whoa, whoa, whoa," interrupted Sim. "Beyond the afterlife? You don't mean that resurrection thing, do you?"

"I do," answered Sarx.

"What's resurrection?" asked Mason.

"It's a thing some of the religious leaders have been teaching as of late," explained Sim. "There's a few–*in my opinion*–rather obscure passages in the sacred book that suggest that those who follow God might come back to life at the end of all things."

"But I thought we just said that when we die our spirits go to be with God in his Kingdom?" said Junia, remembering her time in the Water Kingdom. It had certainly seemed like a spiritual place.

"Okay, let's try this again," said Sarx as he stopped walking and turned to his followers. "There are two spiritual kingdoms in this world: Heaven and Hell. If you align yourselves with me, I will let you join my kingdom in Heaven. If you align yourselves with the dragon or any of the various entities that stand with him, I will let you join his kingdom. If you happen to die–*as all naturally do*–then your spirit will enter into the kingdom that you claimed allegiance to in this life. But when the time is right–*and as to when that time is, I do not know, for the Father won't tell me or anyone else for that matter*–but when the time is right, God will have me physically establish his kingdom here on the earth. And when I do that, all the citizens of Heaven will be given new glorious, imperishable, physical bodies to live in for that new physical kingdom."

"Forgive me, Sarx, but this all sounds a little crazy," said Sim.

"As it should, Sim," said Sarx with an intensity in his voice. "For I have yet to meet a human who truly understands the wonderful power of God. Resurrection life is real and I will prove it before I leave this earth. It is not a form of life that looks like life as you know it now. It is a form of life that will be so foreign to you that you will no longer need marriage or the organs needed for it. It is a form of life in which your body will be indestructible. It is everything you could ever dream of. Have faith and I will show you what it looks like when we are done with our current mission."

A long silence followed Sarx's statement before Junia's words cut through it. "But if you're going to show us what resurrection looks like, doesn't that mean you'll have to die first?" she asked.

Sarx took a deep breath. "Yes," he whispered. "Yes, I will have to die. Horribly, actually. For the kingdom of Heaven is often bought and brought with our suffering."

"No," Mason said firmly. "Surely that won't happen to you. I won't let it! I'll stop whoever gets in the way!"

"Your words carry the heart of a dragon, Mason," warned Sarx. "And you tempt me to become a dragon myself."

"No, never!" exclaimed Mason.

"Then embrace suffering, my friend," said Sarx. "And I will be your example."

Sarx then looked around at all the solemn faces staring back at his. Perhaps his intensity didn't let on how heavy his own words weighed upon himself. His stomach turned as he bent over for a moment. "It's getting late," he said. "Let's set up camp for the night. We've got at least two more days ahead of us before we reach the Southern Mountains."

As Sarx walked off the main road to set up camp, he accidentally stepped on a small snake that he wasn't aware of. It hissed and bit into Sarx's heel, causing him to fall over into a nearby thorn bush which left several long gashes across his forehead.

Sarx groaned in pain as the group ran to him to pull him out of the bush. Judah picked up the snake, which was now dead, and surveyed it.

"I'm alright. I'm okay," said Sarx as they grabbed his hands and pulled him out of the bush. He wiped his forehead with the backside of his hand and witnessed all the blood. "Well, I guess I have been better," he chuckled. He then pulled off his cloak and ripped a long, wide piece of fabric off of it to create a bandana of sorts to wrap around the gashes.

"You're lucky it's not a poisonous snake," said Judah as he walked towards them with the dead serpent. "I've seen a lot of these over the years. Make sure you dress the wound and treat it for infection and you should be fine.

"You know a lot about snakes?" asked Phil.

"I do," answered Judah.

"Alright guys, let's get camp set up for Sarx," Mason interrupted. "Why don't you lie down and take a break Sarx. We'll take care of this."

# CHAPTER 18
## THE ASCENT

After two days of learning, laughing and doing miracles for communities along the way, Sarx and his friends arrived at the Southern Mountains. An unnatural chilly wind blew by them, just as it had by the waterfall when the zombie had appeared–though this wind was even colder. Everyone also felt something like an invisible weight on their shoulders. No one needed to know that this was the gate to Hell in order to perceive that it was not a safe place. The air itself proclaimed it.

"I've got a sick feeling in my stomach," said Jim.

"You and me both," echoed Bart.

"Really?" asked Judah. "You hate climbing that much?"

"You don't feel that?" asked Jim.

# THE ASCENT

"I guess not," replied Judah.

None of them could see it, but a sad expression took over Sarx's face at that comment. He bent over and picked up a large stick to use as a staff of sorts and then turned to his crew. "Come on," he said. "We'll want to be back down before dusk."

As Sarx set his foot on the base of the hill, an earthquake rumbled below them, almost as though the mountain was growling at them. This was followed by a poof of grey cloud appearing at the mountain's summit.

"I think you just rang death's doorbell," said Bart.

"I have," said Sarx. "And I will do it again."

The mountain growled at that comment followed by more smoke.

"Quiet you," said Sarx. And immediately the shaking stopped. It didn't even fade off into the distance—it just stopped. Sarx turned to his startled followers and waved them forward with a nod.

The team began to trudge up the steep mountain slowly and silently. There were no sounds of birds or bugs along the way. Nothing seemed able to survive up here.

Well, that couldn't be right. There was plenty to eat and drink up here—granted the vegetation looked odd. And the air wasn't so thin that you couldn't breathe. So maybe "survive" wasn't the right word. Perhaps it was more like nothing could *thrive* up here. And that must have been the case, for it was at that moment that they saw a sheep standing on a ledge above them, eating some of the strange purple vegetation that grew on the mountainside.

# THE RISE OF THE WATER KINGDOM

The sheep grew stranger upon closer inspection. Its eyes were completely black—not as though they were infected, but as though they were all pupils. The purple grass he was chewing on turned into black mold in his mouth and gushed out of his lips. It was disturbing to watch, especially because his tail wagged happily while he chewed on it.

He stared at Sarx and his friends with those huge black eyes. He didn't move an inch as they approached him, but just kept chewing on his food. The team decided to keep their distance from the sheep, but as they began to look around, they noticed more sheep acting the same way.

Sarx's friends jumped backwards when they noticed a serpent approach the sheep closest to them. Its black and yellow stripes screamed caution, as did the poison dripping from its fangs. It opened its mouth unnaturally wide to consume the sheep, causing the whole group to shudder. And while no one wanted to watch this poor sheep be eaten by the snake, it was also one of those things that was hard to look away from—especially because the weirdest thing happened: As the snake consumed the sheep, the sheep continued to keep its shape inside of the snake. The snake's eyes were where the sheep's eyes belonged and the snake's lips left enough space for the sheep's tongue to look like his own. Yes, as odd as it sounds, "snake-sheep" is the best way to describe the strange hybrid creature standing in front of them.

"You look hungry travelersssss," said the snake-sheep with a deep voice, using the sheep's tongue to speak.

Everyone gasped in horror at the absurdity as they searched for the words to respond to the animal. Bart, of course, was the one who found them first.

"And you look stupid," he said.

"Bart, don't make a creature that poisonous and sentient angry!" warned Matt.

# THE ASCENT

"I mean, he's not wrong though," agreed Mason.

Their insults seemed to bounce right off the snake-sheep. "Care to try some fruit?" it asked as it pushed a strange fruit towards them with its nose. "It'sssss quite deliciousssss."

They didn't have to take a bite to agree. Words fall short of describing what that fruit looked like, but it was certainly the most appetizing thing they had ever seen and they all greatly desired to try it–all except Sarx, that was. True, he might have agreed that it was desirable, but he forced himself to get over that desire so quickly that he was free of temptation in a second. He looked to his friends who all looked in a daze.

"What is that?" asked Thad.

"It'sssss freedom," responded the snake-sheep.

"Freedom?" replied Thad. "Freedom is not a fruit."

"I dissssagree," said the snake-sheep. "What isssss that feeling in your heart right now?"

"That we shouldn't eat that fruit," answered Matt.

"I thought ssssso," said the snake-sheep. "Then your freedom issssss in taking and eating it, isssss it not?"

"That makes sense I sssssuppose," interjected Judah.

Judah's hiss snapped Junia out of her daze. "Why did you say it like that?" she asked.

"Say what?" asked Judah.

"Hissed. You hissed your words like a snake," she pointed out.

At realizing this, all of the others started to shake their heads as though they were coming out of a daydream of sorts. "He did say it like that," said Mason.

"I heard it too," said Jimmy.

Judah then realized that he had, in fact, hissed. "It was a joke! I was mocking the creature!" he defended. His gaze turned to Sarx who carried sorrow in his eyes. "A joke!" he repeated. "It was a joke! Sarx, you believe me!"

Sarx didn't acknowledge his comment. "Why has Judah's hissing pulled you all out of the spell?" he asked the others.

The twelve stopped to ponder this for a moment. "Because he sounded like a reptile I suppose," said Junia.

"A dragon," added Sim.

"And?" asked Sarx.

"Well you said it yourself," said Sim as he glared at Judah. "Those who align themselves with the dragon and his kingdom, go on to be with the dragon in his kingdom."

"Why are you staring at Judah so intently, Sim?" said Sarx. "Are you judging or discerning?"

"Uh," thought Sim. "Judging, if I'm honest… I think."

"Interesting," replied Sarx. "All twelve of you fell into temptation and yet, when you all came back to, you pointed your finger at someone who had the same problem as you."

# THE ASCENT

"But he hissed!" said Jimmy. "He fell more deeply into the trance than we did!"

Sarx let out a heavy sigh. "The blame game tends to follow the shame game. Jimmy, don't point out the shred of lettuce between someone else's teeth when there's an entire carrot lodged between your own."

"It wasn't our fault!" said Phil, blushing. "We were enchanted!"

"Because you allowed yourself to be! And by what? A fruit offered by a hissing striped serpent that ate a demented sheep?" Sarx let out a huge laugh. "I mean, come on guys! A pig could have discerned not to eat that and he would eat anything!"

"Yeah," said Bart. "That's a fair point."

"You don't need your pupils dilated to see clearly," said Sarx. "If the creator wanted your vision to be that widened he would have made you that way. These animals will burn their eyes out in time if they haven't already. They think they have true wisdom and that they claimed it by freeing themselves from God's wisdom, but the truth is that they can't see at all. In the end, all they are is the blind mouthpieces of serpents, waiting for one false step to lead them to their death. So if that's the so-called freedom you desire, take of it and eat. That's your choice. But one last factor of discernment: Keep in mind that this kind of fruit only grows in the kingdom of death."

And with that, Sarx continued up the mountain while his words generally ended the enchantment for everyone. There was no doubt that the fruit looked delicious, but he was right, the discernment was obvious.

"Let's keep moving," Mason said to everyone else as he turned to follow Sarx. They all agreed and turned to move forward.

Judah was the last in line and was the only one to see the snake squeeze the sheep down inside of him until there was nothing left. He stared deep into Judah's eyes for a moment and then slithered away.

"Judah?" called Thad.

"Yeah, I'm coming," Judah called back.

# CHAPTER 19
## THE DRAGON'S LAIR

As they neared the summit of the Southern Mountains, they began to feel hot instead of cold. The air also began to reek of sulfur.

"Fire and brimstone," said Matt. "This must be the gates of Hell."

"Uh, guys?" called Tom with fear in his voice. "Judging by this guy, I'd say, yeah—we're pretty close."

From their left came a tall, large, shadow that was even bigger than the zombie they had encountered a few days earlier. It was probably about six and a half feet tall and looked muscular enough to wear armor that weighed over a hundred pounds. Its shadowy body flickered, occasionally revealing a dim face underneath. Every few seconds you could catch a small glimpse of its knit eyebrows and glaring eyes.

"What are these... these... giants?" asked Matt.

"Some kind of demon, that's for sure," answered Tom.

"It's probably the dead spirits of the giants of old," said Phil.

"Say what now?" asked Mason.

"You know the ancient legends, don't you?" asked Phil.

"I guess not," said Mason.

"What legends?" questioned Junia.

"It's odd how many people miss that story," Phil said to Tom.

"I'm with them, man," said Tom.

Tom sighed. "In the first few chapters of the sacred book there is a story about spiritual beings that married human women and gave birth to the giants."

"What you talking about?" interjected Bart.

"The giants?" said Tom shaking his head at blank faces. "Like the giant the great king of old defeated with a slingshot?"

"That was much later than the first few chapters of the sacred book," said Jimmy, fearfully backing away from another giant that was silently walking towards him from a different direction.

"Come on people, they're all throughout the book!" said Tom. "Early on, the Creator sent a hurricane to wipe them out, but then they reappeared later among all kinds of people groups. They were the reason for the holy wars our ancestors fought! And they were only still around in the time of the great

King because the Creator's people stopped following their mission to remove them."

"Apparently I need to read the sacred book again," said Bart as he moved away from a group of shades that were slowly approaching them from behind.

"So you're telling us that these things are those giants?" asked Junia.

"Well, that's what public speculation would suggest," answered Tom. "I mean, what are they? They're not fully human. They're not fully spirit. They're not the intentional creation of God, but the creation of inferior spiritual beings that God created. They're the product of divine rebellion and so they lived like rebels while they were on the earth. They don't belong in Heaven, but perhaps the dragon of Hell doesn't keep them bound there either. And so they roam the earth as demons."

Their entire group had slowly come together in a huddle as the shades closed in on them on all sides but the front. It was clear from the way they were approaching that they were intentionally pushing their crew towards the summit, where they had seen the poofs of smoke arise earlier.

"So demons are the disembodied souls of the giants then?" asked Mason.

"Well, yes and no," replied Tom. "Lots of things can be qualified as a demon– the sons of God, the little-g-gods, fallen angels, the spiritual powers that be, and yes, the giants. Basically, if it's a spiritual being in opposition to God, you could identify it under the blanket term, 'demon,' even though it may have a different story as to how it became a demon. These particular ones in front of us right now, I imagine, are the spirits of the dead giants."

Their group was forced by the giant shades further and further into the clouds where things grew hotter and hotter. They were now yards away from the top. Then feet. Then inches. Then...

"It's a volcano," said Jim.

In front of them was a giant caldera that stretched for miles around. Directly at their feet was a long stairs that descended deep into the volcano and led to an island of sorts surrounded by lava. The island was rich with the same kind of purple vegetation they had seen the sheep eat. And not only that, but there was a tree there that, though it appeared dead, was full of the fruit they had all been enchanted by earlier. Though that fruit looked a little less appealing while hanging on such an ugly tree.

A large golden throne the size of a two-story house took up much of the island. It was bedazzled with every possible jewel you could think of and some you could only imagine. It glimmered and shined in the bright red light of the lava.

Upon the throne sat the dragon himself: The Plaintiff—and most of Sarx's crew would agree that he was the most beautiful creature they had ever seen. Gazing upon him was like gazing upon the most seductive person you could imagine. It was as though they couldn't pull their minds off of his beauty—*let alone their eyes*. This, of course, sounds very odd, for he was in fact a dragon. But rather than scream at the sight of the titan, they were more enamored with him.

Behind the throne was a very wide path that led to very wide gates which were as beautiful as the dragon himself. Any human would instantly try to get a closer look had they caught a glimpse of the gates from a distance. Sarx's friends gathered that these must be the gates of Hell.

Two shadowy angel-like beings stood on each side of the gate, but something seemed a bit backwards about them. It seemed as though they weren't interested in protecting their kingdom from intrusion, but rather that they were trying to keep their residents inside. This must have been the case, because judging by the weeping on the other side of the doors, someone certainly didn't want to be in there.

Suddenly, a sound hard to describe came from the shades. They were closing in on them, pushing them towards the long winding stairs that led down into the volcano. Sarx placed his walking stick on the step in front of him and then proceeded down the stairs. As he did, the dragon looked up at him, smirked, and let out a low and earthshaking growl. Rings of smoke exited out of his nostrils as he breathed, each making their way up out of the volcano and into the clouds.

"Sssssarxxxxxxx," the dragon's slow, low voice rumbled through the volcano. He was easily a mile away, but everyone could hear him as though he was standing right next to them. "Come. Let ussss talk."

The dragons wings flew out of his back and were an incredible sight to behold. The demons all around the volcano cheered and hissed and cackled, sending shivers down the spines of Sarx's friends.

"Into the fires of Hell itself," said Phil as he wiped the sweat from his forehead and followed the others.

"He took on an army of demons by himself," Mason reminded. "We'll be fine."

"Will we?" asked Junia.

Mason looked to his sister with strong, but questionable eyes. He managed a small smile and nodded, letting out a slight hum.

# THE DRAGON'S LAIR

Lava bubbles popped far below them, sending little droplets of lava in all directions. The heat was so intense that it felt like it sucked every droplet of water out of their skin. But they noticed the closer they stayed to Sarx, the more bearable it was.

They walked silently down the steps as all kinds of beings and spirits taunted them and cursed at them—many of their eyes dilated like the sheep's, and their teeth sharp and black as poison. They proclaimed the praises of the dragon as they approached him and they spit on Sarx as he walked by.

Finally, after a long walk down, they were face to face with the Plaintiff himself. And it was there that Sarx's friends noticed two things–(1) two keys hung on a chain around the dragon's neck and (2), the dragon's legs and wings weren't real. They were metallic and built out of some kind of futuristic technology of sorts. They moved and worked like real legs, but they definitely weren't. The Plaintiff had clearly been severely handicapped at some point in his long life.

As they finally reached the island, the dragon pulled his long tail out of the lava. He moved it swiftly and hot lava flew from it, hitting some of the beasts in the volcano. They screeched as it burned them. He leaned forward in his throne and spit a rather large bone out of his mouth.

"Sssssson of God," the Plaintiff addressed the small man in front of him. "Well you certainly have some guts coming here. Especially after attacking my kingdom so recently. You've nearly rid me of an entire country and now I must punish my soldiers until they are encouraged enough to try to take it again. You also injured the water beast shortly before that. Needless to say, I am not in a good mood. So for what do I owe thisss pleasssssure? You're far too early for the final battle, are you not?"

Sarx stood silently in front of him.

"Hmm. A man of few words. I like that. It gives me more time to speak–and oh how I love to sssssspeak. And I especially love to speak when I see a group of misfits sssuch as thesssssse."

The Plaintiff took note of Sarx's team who stood fearfully behind him as a devious smile came over his face. Metallic spikes came out of his long neck as it curved around Sarx. His large eye met Junia's ear. She shivered, but she refused to turn to look at the beautifully disgusting creature. She closed her eyes and grasped her brother's hand tightly.

"Kahli," the dragon's low voice softly boomed. "We've missed you dear. Don't you miss us? You look unwell, child–a little pale. And dare I ask if you've put on some weight?" A tear dropped from Junia's eye as her lips curled into a horrible shape.

"That's enough!" yelled Mason, inciting the screams and howls of many Hellish creatures. The dragon's neck moved lightning fast from one side of Junia to the other side of Mason.

"Don't you talk to me like that you little heart-breaker," he roared, small flames exiting through his teeth. "Yessssss, your life is full of holiness isn't it?"

"Holiness is a quality my Father gives to the people and things that belong to him. It is not a quality that can be earned through morality," Sarx interjected calmly, causing the dragon to pull his neck back to see him. "But of course, you knew that at one point, didn't you?"

The dragon huffed a large smoke ring directly over the crew and then plummeted his metal claw right in front of Sarx, narrowly missing his foot. He stuck out his metallic wings as fire filled his veins. "Your Father took my feet from me and threw me down to this dissssgusting planet! Do you think I care about holinessssss?"

"This is why you make a bad Plaintiff," replied Sarx, still keeping his calm. "Your heart is filled with hated and it clouds your courtroom skills. You accuse left and right, forgetting about the heart of the judge you are trying to persuade."

The dragon let out a deep laugh. "I don't need to convince the judge of humanity's wickedness. I just need to convince humanity that they are evil—a little accusation here and a little accusation there—a little temptation here and a little temptation there. It doesn't take long before they've accused themselves so much that they can't break out of their own shame, causing them to spiral further out of control to try to break their depression. Humans are sssssimple-minded creaturesssss, desperate to think and to act on their own terms in their own way. My associates have been trying to show your Father that for centuries! If the Creator were to stop treating humans so well, every last one of them would turn against him. But he is too foolish to see that."

"Really?" said Sarx. "The Creator of true wisdom is foolish?"

The dragon knit his brows and snorted hot smoke out of his nostrils. "He issssss. If only he wasn't so blinded by his lovesssssicknessssss, he would agree. Then he would see the validity of every last accusation I could make on all of your friends here. Then he would see the death that creeps under their very skin, edging them into complete wickedness."

Sarx shook his head. "Your pride has always been the most destructive thing about you, Daystar. And after all of these centuries, it still is."

The Plaintiff stuck his nose right up next to Sarx, his mouth bigger than Sarx's entire body. "What… do you… want?" he glared.

Sarx walked away from the Plaintiff's mouth and grabbed Mason's shoulder and took him to the center of the volcanic island. He then took off his blood soaked-bandana, tied it to his walking stick, and placed it in Mason's hands. The dragon sat back in his throne and raised an eyebrow in intrigue. Sarx slowly looked around the volcano at all the beasts and spirits as a stillness filled the air in anticipation of whatever it was that he was about to do.

"I come with a message from the kingdom of Heaven," Sarx boldly yelled across the volcano. "Here in this place, I anoint Mason to build my Kingdom—and Hell will be unable to stop my citizens." Sarx then grabbed Mason's hands and used them to shove the sharp edge of his walking stick—*now turned into a blood-soaked flag*—deep into the Southern Mountains.

At once the entire kingdom of Hell let out a terrifying screech as the Plaintiff stretched out his metallic wings, and threw his head back and blew flames high into the air.

Immediately the Spirit of Light whisked Sarx and the twelve away.

# CHAPTER 20
## The Inn

"We need to find a place to stay before everywhere closes," said Sarx as he rapidly made his way through the dark forest towards the city ahead of them.

"Wait a minute," called Matt. "Where even are we? How did we get here?"

"The Spirit has granted us a miracle," answered Sarx still pushing through the tree branches.

"You mean we could fly places all this time and yet we hiked an entire mountain?" exclaimed Bart.

"The conversation is not that simple Bart," Sarx said as he exited the forest, the others soon joining him.

The sun was setting over the town and all of its residents appeared to be heading home for the night. Sarx saw an inn not far from them and ran to it.

# THE INN

He knocked loudly until a slot in the door opened up, revealing a man's eyes behind it. The man surveyed Sarx and his ragtag group of sweaty, dirty, beat-up followers. You didn't have to see his full facial expression to know what he was thinking. His eyes revealed it all.

"We're full up," he lied.

"We have money, friend," smiled Sarx.

"Not enough, *friend*," the man responded sarcastically as he closed the slot.

"Hey!" yelled Jimmy. "Do you know where we've been today?"

"And what we've done?" yelled Johnny.

"I don't think he does!" laughed Jimmy.

"Oh, I know he doesn't!" Johnny added. "And there's no way he could ever guess how we got here!"

"I'm still questioning how we got here!" Jimmy laughed.

"We've witnessed all kinds of crazy things in the last few days, so how about you open up before we call down fire on this place!" yelled Johnny.

"Jimmy! Johnny! That's enough!" scolded Sarx. "What is this? You meet the dragon for a brief moment and then you become one yourself? How dare you invoke the kingdom of love with such thunder in your voice! Calm yourselves!"

"Yes sir," the brothers replied sheepishly.

"This man said he's full up," Sarx said. "I've basically been denied a place to stay since the day I was born. Let's just move along to the next city and find a different one."

"Or you could come rest at my place," said a voice from behind the group.

Sarx turned around and his face lit up. "Marie!" he greeted as the two exchanged a hug and a smile. "It's been quite some time! How is the family?"

Immediately her face fell. "Oh, not so well," Marie said, trying to hold back tears.

Sarx's voice grew cold and quiet. "What's wrong?"

An eerie silence filled the air as a knot filled both of their stomachs. Marie looked to the ground and began to sob.

# CHAPTER 21
## Nico

The thirteen of them made their way through the darkened streets to Marie's house where her family and friends had been grieving. As the door opened, Marie's sister, Marsha, caught one glimpse of Sarx and immediately started bawling. She cupped her hand around her face as Sarx slowly sat down next to her. He put his arm around her to comfort her, causing her to weep uncontrollably, her tears soaking his clothes. Then, just as quickly as she had leaned into his embrace, she pulled away and started slapping him on the chest with both hands as though angry.

"Where were you?" she asked, every word separated by gasps for air. "The man guided by God's very voice? The man empowered by God's very Spirit? What? Does God not have time for me? Does he not hear my cries? Was someone else's healing so much more important than the death of my brother and your friend? And now you show up three days late? Does God not know what time it is?"

She looked into Sarx's hurt eyes and immediately felt guilty. Her mouth opened wide as she cried from the back of her throat and plummeted her face into his chest. Sarx put his arm around her back as his body began to slowly shake with his own cries—each breath forced out of his nose in a very sorrowful way. The room grew quiet for a brief moment before the silence was broken by Sarx's loud inhale, followed by more shaking and weeping from both of them. Marie sat down behind her sister and hugged her close, putting her head on her shoulder. She, too, began to cry.

Eventually everyone in the room was moved by the grief and either teared up or joined in the grieving. It generated such a commotion that many of the houses in the neighborhood took notice. People left their homes in the middle of the night to make sure that everyone was okay. The crowd grew and grew as the community caught wind of the fact that the famous healer was in their town.

They all looked on as Sarx cried. He had yet to say a word since he arrived. But within time, he was able to regain some composure. His hands then curled into fists and he looked to the sisters.

"Show me Nico's grave," he said with a sniff.

Marsha took a handkerchief and wiped the tears from her eyes and pointed towards the window. "It's right outside," she said.

Sarx stood up and began to walk towards the front door. The crowd parted to the left and right as he did, everyone curious to see what he would do. His face could be seen just enough in the light of the crowd's lamps to note the tears in his eyes. When he reached the grave, he took a shovel from nearby and started to dig.

"What are you doing?" Marsha cried. "Haven't we been through enough? Now you desecrate his grave?"

Sarx continued to dig with vigor. "Your brother will be raised back to life," he said as he grunted with each hole he made.

Marsha's weeping burst out her mouth like air stuck in her lips. "Now's not the time for one of your lessons, Sarx."

"It's not a lesson, Marsha," said Sarx as he continued to dig, a few of his followers joining him in the process. Some of the others seemed to agree that it was desecration and were too afraid to offend.

"Sure it's not," Marsha cried. "Look, I get it—we'll be raised in the last days when the kingdom comes to earth. We'll be given new bodies and all that. I believe you—you don't need to make a scene to make your point. He's gone now and I just need to grieve. Please cover him up!"

*Crack!* Sarx's shovel hit the coffin. Marsha threw her hand over her eyes and wept once again. His friends quickly uncovered the rest of the coffin and after a few gasps, the crowd—and even the crickets—fell completely silent.

And there in the dead of night in front of the whole community, Sarx bent down and said, "Nico. Get up."

Immediately the covering of the coffin was kicked off from the inside and Nico sat up and inhaled a mighty breath. Marsha and Marie immediately bolted to the grave and began to help their brother out as he coughed heavily. The crowd became so loud that it woke up everyone in the neighborhood and even the nearest city. The news began to spread like wildfire.

Sarx smiled and then gazed into the empty coffin where shadowy dragon-like eyes glared back at him before disappearing.

While the crowd rejoiced at the wonders of God, Sarx pulled his friends aside. "Our time is short," he said. "This news will set in motion the final chain of events. For not all in this crowd are rejoicing with us."

Sarx nodded the direction of some of the religious leaders. One of them cleared his throat and spit and then turned around and walked into the darkness.

"Tomorrow we make our way to the sacred city–to Old Salem herself. Be alert. Be awake. Be ready," warned Sarx. "The Plaintiff has puppets in every part of society–especially among the powers, whether they be state or religion."

"The religious leaders?" asked Phil. "That doesn't make any sense–they're the good guys!"

"Sheep under snakeskin," said Sarx. "Be alert. Be awake. Be ready."

# CHAPTER 22
## Old Salem

"May I borrow this donkey, sir?" asked Bart. "I'll bring it right back, but I work with Sarx and he is in need of it for now."

The man stared at Bart with a strange expression.

"Yes?" asked Bart. "That looks like a yes. I'm going to take that as a yes." Bart then grabbed the donkey and walked out the front gates of Old Salem while the man stared on without saying anything. "He said yes, I think," Bart told the gang while Sarx mounted the donkey.

"Time for the king to enter his kingdom," Johnny whispered to Jimmy.

"Where we'll be his righthand men," Jimmy said raising his eyebrows and slapping Johnny's hand.

Though it was impossible that Sarx would have heard them, he turned to them as though he did. "You still don't know what you're getting into, do you? You do not know the cup you are asking to drink, but it will be offered to you." The two of them hung their heads low as Sarx looked at them, but when Sarx looked away they looked back at each other and smiled.

The donkey then made its way into the gates of Old Salem, immediately grabbing the attention of everyone present. The city was packed for the most sacred holiday of the year and the smell of roasted lamb filled the air.

"That's the guy who brought that one guy back to life," a woman whispered.

"I heard he came out of a giant fish and just started healing people," another man said.

"They say he's going to bring God's kingdom back," another man said. "That he'll revive Old Salem!"

"You mean install New Salem!" corrected a woman.

"I heard that he's got royalty in his blood," said another woman. "Descended from the great king of old himself."

"All hail King Sarx!" a man cried from across the street.

"All hail King Sarx!" a woman replied from elsewhere.

"All hail King Sarx!" yelled three children in front of Sarx's donkey.

Soon everyone was gathering around and calling out praises to God and to his new king. A man started singing a holiday song and all of the crowd joined in as they began to inaugurate Sarx with a makeshift parade, right in front of the kings that already existed and the religious leaders who desired to see his demise.

In that moment, the praises of God's people were louder than they had been in a long time. And at the same time, the spiritual weight of the atmosphere was heavier than it had *ever* been. And there was not a moment that Sarx could not feel it pressing down on his shoulders.

Eventually, Sarx and his group reached a home in which they were given a space to celebrate the holidays. Sarx dismounted his humble donkey and waved goodbye to everyone and then went inside to prepare dinner. While he did so the gang broke up for a bit to enjoy the festivities of the day.

# CHAPTER 23
## THE HOLIDAY FEAST

Sarx's friends later returned to the house and met in the living room to discuss the day's events. They were pumped up like never before.

"I can't believe it's happening!" shouted Tom as he raised a glass. "New Salem is almost here!"

"Here, here!" yelled the others as they clanked their glasses together.

"Just think: In time we'll be ruling this city," smiled Johnny.

"Associates of God's one true king!" exclaimed Jimmy.

"It is amazing to think of it that way," nodded Mason.

"I would certainly say so," said Matt. "One second you're lost in a forest with a dying sister and the next you're working for royalty. Now that's an underdog story if I ever heard one."

"Do you think it's quite that simple though?" asked Junia sheepishly.

"What do you mean?" asked Thad.

"You know," she replied. "Installing the kingdom and all that?"

"Well let's recap, shall we?" Phil broke in. "We're following a man that calls himself the Son of Man; that demons call the Son of God; who strikes fear into armies of demons; who controls the waves; who has the power to raise the dead; and has the audacity to march into Hell itself and plant a flag. I'm sorry, how much more simple could it be? The guy is unbeatable!"

"I don't disagree with that," replied Junia. "You'll remember that we've been with him longer than the rest of you and have seen other crazier things he's done that you haven't."

"Then what do you mean?" asked Jim.

Junia let out a sigh as she twirled her drink with her hand. "I mean the things you all keep ignoring. Like earlier today, Jimmy and Johnny were told that they didn't know what they were getting into. They were also scolded when they threatened to burn a place to the ground with supernatural power. And Mason: Sarx thought that your passion might be used the wrong way when you pledged your life to his cause, right after telling Sophroneo he had no need for a body guard. And unless I misunderstood, I think he told us directly that he was going to die. I feel like there's been other strange expressions he's made too, I just can't remember them all."

"I think you're looking into all of this a bit much," said Matt. "The man speaks in mysteries half the time. There's probably just some metaphorical meaning behind those things he said."

"But what if there's not?" she asked. "What if this kingdom of his isn't anything like… like… like what we've always expected it to be?"

Junia's statement was followed by a long silence, which meant it was the perfect time for Bart to cut in with a well-timed joke. But what he had to say wasn't the kind of commentary anyone expected from him.

"I mean, she could be right," he said. "Like you said yourself Phil, he just walked into Hell and planted his flag. I hope I'm wrong, but I imagine that has repercussions. I'd, too, like to hope that things go the way we've expected and that we completely overthrow our oppressors and install the kingdom as soon as tomorrow, but–"

Bart's words were cut off by the squeak of a door. Sarx came through it with a towel around his arm and a bowl of water in his hands. He was wearing no shirt and looked like a common slave. And if he didn't feel humiliated, his friends sure felt humiliated for him. Several tried to look away.

"But then there's moments like this," continued Bart.

"If you wish to be a part of what I'm doing, you must let me serve you and wash your feet," Sarx said.

Everyone stared blankly and a few mumbled something.

"You've all been cleaned in the waters of the kingdom already, but you have kicked up a bit of dirt upon yourselves since. I must remove it. And you must continue to let me remove it every time. And as I take on the posture of a slave for you, so you must take on this posture for others. For it is the lowly slaves of this world that are the princes of the next one. So choose temporary slavery now if you wish to have a greater return in my Father's kingdom."

Mason stood up slowly and made his way to Sarx, causing the rest to reluctantly follow. Judah was the only one who didn't get up from his spot. "I don't feel well," he said when his turn came. His face was hot and cold at the same time and his stomach turned.

"Then I'll come there," said Sarx as he sat on the ground in front of him and began to wash his feet. Judah turned away and felt like he was going to throw up.

Sarx finished the ritual and invited everyone to sit at the dinner table for the holiday feast. It was a time full of traditions that all around the table knew well and followed almost without thinking.

First, a cup of wine was brought to the table and Sarx picked it up and said a blessing over it. After this, the night's meal was laid out on the table, and the appetizers were eaten. You could tell by the joyful noises everyone made that it was quite delicious.

Next, a second cup of wine was poured and Sarx began to tell the holiday story that they all knew quite well.

"You'll recall that our people were once slaves under an oppressive nation," he said. "But God came to our aid and made us free women and men. He poured out his righteous judgment upon our oppressors and their gods in attempts to get them to let us go. But their king was a stiff-necked king and it took harsh judgment to break him. His firstborn, along with all the firstborns of his nation—human or animal—were taken. But we all painted the blood of a sacrificial lamb on the doors of our houses. And when God saw that blood, he passed over our houses and let us live."

Then Sarx threw everyone for a loop when he broke from the traditional story. For instead of identifying the foods in front of them in the holiday ways that everyone expected, he gave them new meaning. He picked up a piece of bread, broke it, and said, "I am the bread of life and I will suffer and be broken for you. Eat this in remembrance of me."

Everyone looked around, waiting to see who would eat it first. The whole thing didn't sit well with them—Judah especially. But finally they ate, Mason once again in the lead.

Judah gripped his stomach tightly as it gurgled so loudly everyone could hear it. Everyone looked to him as a frown came over Sarx's face.

"Do not think I haven't noticed your dilated pupils, Judah," Sarx said. "Or that I am not aware that you took the fruit of Hell from the snake-sheep while we were there. Or that I have no idea about the plot you made with the religious officials today."

Judah looked into Sarx's eyes, but everything was so bright that he could hardly see. His pupils were three times the size of everyone else's. His head spun and Sarx became blurry and doubled in his vision.

"It appears you have already decided on this matter," Sarx said. He then leaned close to Judah and stared into his lifeless eyes, which, for a moment, were replaced by the very eyes of the Plaintiff. A snake like tongue hissed from his mouth as a devious smile overtook his face."

"Do what you came here to do and do it quickly," Sarx said with little inflection in his voice. Judah looked down the table as his eyes grew entirely black. He then ran out the door as a snake opened its mouth and immediately took over his body.

# THE HOLIDAY FEAST

Mason stood up to ask for an explanation about what had just happened, but Sarx's gaze was locked onto the cooked lamb on the table. Suddenly, Sarx snapped back to and looked at Mason with heavy eyes.

"I'm sorry, what did you say, Mason?" he asked.

"Shouldn't we go after him?" Mason asked. "If he's eaten of the Dragon's fruit, aren't we all in danger?"

"We will deal with danger in time," Sarx replied. "For now, we have a feast to finish. And where were we in that feast?" Sarx gazed around the table. "Ah yes, the end of the second cup. I believe it's time to sing the customary hymns."

Sarx led the tune and poured out the third cup while the rest of the table joined him with solemn and distracted voices. It was impossible to forget what had just happened and many of them felt a tangible fear enter their bones.

But after the third cup had been poured, everyone ate the meal and entered into lively conversation. Sarx smiled and nodded here and there, but he still struggled to break his gaze away from the lamb on the table. After they had finished and were quite stuffed, Sarx then drew their attention to the third cup he had poured earlier.

"God is making a new promise to you through me," he said. "You have already eaten of my body. Now you must drink of my blood, which will provide the new promise for you."

This, of course, was even more disconcerting than the bread, but each of them partook just the same. Then a fourth cup was poured and the table entered into another time of singing. Finally the time came to drink the fourth cup and end the holiday meal. But just as Sarx had changed a few of the components of the night, so he changed this one.

"We will not be drinking the fourth cup right now," he explained. "For it is the most bitter cup of all and it will require great strength to partake of it. I pray that I somehow will not have to drink of it, but I do not see another way." His gaze was drawn once again to the lamb on the table, nothing left of it but its bones.

"Pray for me," Sarx requested, as blood suddenly dripped from one of the scars in his forehead. He picked up a napkin and dabbed the wound. "Pray that my Father's will be done, no matter how hard it may seem. For when all is said and done, I will partake of this final cup in God's kingdom with you all as we eat of the greatest marriage feast ever cooked. It is there that this cup will be turned from bitter into sweet. It is then that God's new promise will reach its completion and his kingdom will be fully established on the earth. It is then that he will pass over all of the houses of the earth with his righteous judgment and spare all of those who have painted the blood of my body on the doors of their hearts. Then, we may finally close out this holiday meal with the cup of all cups."

"Here, here!" said Jimmy.

"Here, here!" the rest chimed in.

Junia noticed the sudden change in demeanor. The talk of the kingdom had amped them all up again to the point that they seemed to instantly forget the incredibly bitter conversations of the last two hours.

"Our time here has grown short," said Sarx. "As I said last night, the final chain of events has been put into motion. And that motion will scatter you all from me."

"What?" gasped Mason. "I would never leave you. I'm sorry but you're stuck with me," he smiled as he crossed his arms.

Sarx gave Mason a dim smile. "Again, I appreciate your passion Mason. But you still misunderstand kingdom tactics. And when you do finally get it, you will not only scatter from me, but deny having ever known me."

"No," said Mason. "No, I wouldn't."

A tear fell from Sarx's cheek as he nodded. "But you will." He then looked out the window into total darkness. Not even the moon could be seen. "The time is here now. We must leave."

# CHAPTER 24
## THE GARDEN

It was there in a garden that Judah reappeared alongside some religious leaders and their servants. There was also as a group of soldiers carrying weapons and torches so that they could see in the incredible darkness. Judah's hood covered his face so that it was difficult to see the snake underneath. Sarx's friends, who had been struggling to stay awake suddenly leapt to their feet and took on a defensive stature.

"What's happening?" called Phil.

"The start of the great war, perhaps?" said Johnny.

"He did say the time was short. Maybe this is the moment," said Jimmy.

Mason began to ponder their words.

"Guys, I think you're still misunderstanding," interjected Junia.

# THE GARDEN

"Well come on now," said Matt. "He's taken on a demonic army, he can handle these few."

Sarx's face remained expressionless as his cloak and hair blew in the cold wind.

"How can I help you?" asked Sarx, addressing all of the soldiers but staring straight at Judah who quickly looked away.

"We are looking for a self-proclaimed king from a small town who entered Old Salem today. Goes by the name, Sarx," responded a guard. "Are you him?"

Sarx nodded slowly and replied, "*I am.*"

Immediately the Spirt of Light burst out of him in all directions, causing the soldiers to draw back and fall to the ground. Sarx slowly approached the confused soldiers.

"How can I help you?" he asked again.

"Uh," said the chief guard as he pulled himself up, confused as to what had just happened. "We… we are looking for a man named Sarx."

"I told you, that's who *I am*," replied Sarx, as the Spirit of Light pushed the guard once again. "Let my friends go and I will come with you."

As soon as Sarx had made this statement he heard a loud yell from the trees. Mason popped out behind a servant with a sword in hand. The servant turned to see what was happening, throwing off Mason's aim in the process and causing him to slice the servant's ear off. The man fell to the ground, yelling in pain and cupped his hand around his ear to hold in the blood.

## THE RISE OF THE WATER KINGDOM

Sarx looked directly at Mason with intensity burning in his eyes. "What have you done?" he asked.

"I told you I wouldn't betray you!" Mason cried.

"Is that what you were doing all day while I was preparing dinner? You were out buying a sword? The kind of sword I explicitly told you you wouldn't need in ministry when I sent you out to do miracles with your sister?" asked Sarx with a raised voice.

Sarx shook his head as Mason looked down at the poor servant. "But I—"

"You have disobeyed my instructions and taken a pot shot at a poor slave. A slave of all people, which I just told you hours ago that you are to live like in order to be great in the kingdom!" yelled Sarx.

"Well how am I supposed to storm the gates of Hell and build your kingdom there without a weapon!" Mason yelled back in confusion. "I'll be killed the moment I walk in!"

"As I told you before: In your passion you have misunderstood the kingdom of Heaven," answered Sarx.

"You said I had to be all in! I'm all in right now!" yelled Mason in confusion.

"Yes, *all in* because you very well may have to lay down your life for the cause at the hands of your oppressors, *for your oppressors*. For the kingdom is often bought with blood—not theirs, but your own! This is the tactics of Heaven. And should you have been paying attention like your sister, you would have noticed this by now."

Sarx then dropped to his knees and picked up the slave's ear. He shushed the poor man, saying, "All will be well in a moment." He then pressed the ear to the man's head and prayed. Immediately the ear was reconnected and the man was healed, causing everyone to gasp in disbelief.

He then looked one last time at Mason. "We put body parts back on people. We never take them off. We do not stoop to the level of the dragon in order to fight the dragon. When we do so, even in our victory we have already lost and perpetuated the kingdom of hate, installing it deeper into every country we enter. We fight by laying down our lives. Now I see that you are willing to die for me if you can hold a weapon. Are you willing to die for me without one?" Sarx then grabbed Mason's arm and pulled up his sleeve. "You're growing scales, Mason."

Mason's eyes began to swell up with tears as he was overcome with terror. Scales? He was becoming a dragon? And what could he do to the gates of Hell without a sword? How would Sarx become king without an army? How did anything make sense without some kind of weapon? Anxiety overcame him as he dropped his sword and ran into the forest as fast as he could.

Sarx turned to Junia. "Take care of him," he nodded. The others also turned and ran away, scattering across the forest. The Kingdom of Heaven was now becoming real to them for the first time.

Sarx was now alone with the dragon's many puppets. And despite the evening's displays of power, they were still all too blinded by the Plaintiff to let Sarx go. Sarx watched as a religious official handed Judah some money and in that very moment the snake encompassing him spit him out. He then crawled up to Judah's ear and whispered, "Ssssssshame," and slithered away.

The guards grabbed Sarx and led him away, leaving Judah standing there with his cash. His pupils suddenly returned to a normal size as the coins slipped through his fingers and crashed to the ground with an unexpected thunk.

## THE RISE OF THE WATER KINGDOM

A cold wind swept by him and immediately he knew the Plaintiff was near. A metallic claw reached out from behind him and placed the sword that Mason had dropped into Judah's hand.

*You don't deserve to live*, said the shadow over his shoulder.

# CHAPTER 25
## THE RELIGIOUS LEADERS

Candles lit up the large room that Sarx now stood in as a prisoner. The place felt familiar to him but fake at the same time–as though the room was trying to resemble something ancient and sacred, but had failed completely. It didn't matter how much the architecture got it right–it was the atmosphere that was wrong. The air was stale and tasteless and carried the same spiritual weight that Hell did. It stunk.

"I hope my guards didn't rough you up too much on the way over," said a man at the top of the stairs–clearly the ring leader of the group. "But then again, if they did, I can't help but feel that you probably deserved it."

"Is this the way of a priest these days?" asked Sarx. "Are they all ruffians who pull people out of the dark while they're praying?"

"It is our way when it has to be," the man replied. "And it seems that with you, *it has to be.*"

"Why is that?" asked Sarx.

"Numerous reasons, really," the man replied. "Your teaching for one. It's off-putting. You're a radical who garners more of a crowd everyday around faulty doctrines. You're worse than any of the other denominations out there, for you do not conform to anyone's teaching in full. You're a heretic." He then lunged forward into Sarx's face while the soldiers continued to hold him. "Tell me, Sarx. What exactly is the basis of this teaching of yours?"

"Why did you need to arrest me to figure that out?" asked Sarx. "Just ask anyone I've ministered to and you'll get an answer. I'm not sneaking around spreading teaching like some heretic. I'm preaching it from the stage in Godly places. If there was a problem, surely I wouldn't have been able to teach so frequently."

A soldier slapped Sarx across the face, leaving a red mark so bright that his fingertips could be seen. "Is that how you talk to a priest?" asked the soldier.

Sarx blinked and widened his eyes as though it would erase the sting. "Is that how you act when someone tells you the truth?" he responded.

"Your teaching is full of lies," said the priest. "You speak against us, the very people trying to save the world and pave the way for God's kingdom! We live lives of righteousness and teach others to do the same—following every command and every law so that we can beckon in God's return! We lost God's presence with our great sin—but now we will earn it back with great morality."

Sarx laughed slowly. "Great morality? The sacred book has a heart! It's living and breathing and speaking! But you treat it like magic! As though following rules to a fault will turn your life into an incantation that beckons in the kingdom of God! But your capacity to meet expectations means nothing if you cannot appeal to the book's heart. All of your skills and disciplines equate to nothing more than a deadman's bones in an expensive coffin. Granted, you look nice–*and you certainly trot your beauty around for all to see*–but you have no heart. And if love cannot be found in you, then you have no part in the kingdom of God, let alone the ability to usher it into this world. You are full of judgment and hate, and you not only hold our people up to a heartless interpretation of our book, but you also place on them the weight of doctrines you yourself came up with and teach them as though they were the word of the Creator himself! Is your pride never-ending? And what's more–you pervert the law to your gain! You've become rich with the blood-soaked cash of the poor! And rather than house the poor, you've twisted the Scriptures to grant you the ability to steal their homes!"

"How dare you!" the priest roared as the soldiers shook him.

"How dare I? How dare you turn my Father's house into a den of thieves!"

"Oh, God is your Father now is he?" laughed the priest.

"You would recognize it were so if you weren't so blinded by your own father, the dragon!" Sarx scolded.

The priest's face turned beat red. "Get him out of my sight!" he screamed as the guards pulled Sarx down the hallway.

"Sentence me if you will, but in the end, you will see me high and lifted up for all to see!" Sarx said as he was dragged away.

And with that, the doors closed behind him, the noise reverberating throughout the hall for sometime. After a moment, a handful of priests came out from behind the pillars in the room.

"He is too powerful," said the lead priest.

## THE RELIGIOUS LEADERS

"If we let him go, he will destroy everything we've worked to build. His following is too large," said another.

"Yesssss," hissed the lead priest. "He musssssst die. It's time to ask for a favor from the real king around here."

# CHAPTER 26
## EXECUTION

"He'll do something," said Jimmy as he walked through the mob of people with a scarf and a hood covering his face.

"He has to, right?" asked Johnny. "I mean, I get it now—we really didn't understand this whole kingdom thing. But we can hardly install Heaven in Old Salem—*let alone the earth*—if the king of Heaven is dead."

Sarx and two other men were being pushed through the city by two guards who were whipping and mocking them, leaving large open wounds across their backs. "Come see the inauguration of your king!" they yelled. "Join the parade and celebrate!"

One of the prisoners leaned over to Sarx. "Come on now King—don't think I haven't heard of ya. You're that miracle worker, yeah? Get us out of here already! Make us invisible or something! Use your magic!"

# EXECUTION

Sarx walked silently through the crowd, grunting as the whip hit his back.

The prisoner laughed. "Yeah, you're a joke. Just a dead man like the rest of us."

"Would you shut up!" yelled the other prisoner. "This is a holy man in front of you who hasn't done anything wrong, and yet you mock him? Have you no fear of God? You and I—we deserve this punishment. But this man—*this King*—has been unjustly treated."

The cruel prisoner cleared his throat and spit. Sarx turned to the kind prisoner and managed to give him a small smile while blood poured down his back. Sarx's eye was bruised from an earlier ruckus with the guards and the slap of the solider from the night before had turned into a bruise as well. He was a mess. But despite Sarx's lowly appearance, the prisoner put his fist to his chest and bowed his head. "Hail King Sarx," he said.

"Find me after I join you in my Kingdom," smiled Sarx. "I'll give you a tour of paradise." He then let out a loud grunt as the whip cracked across his back once again.

A woman broke out of the crowd with a crown she had made out of thorns and yelled, "All hail King Sarx!" She then jammed it into his skull, cutting open the scars that were already there and creating new ones as well. The mob cheered. She then spit on his face and ran back to crowd and laughed loudly.

"Forgive them Father. They are all blind to the truth," whispered Sarx. He turned behind him to see a vision of the demons who were pulling the strings behind their soldier puppets.

Finally, they reached their destination: A stadium-sized cage with a forest inside. The three prisoners were shoved inside and the door was locked behind them. The crowd gathered around the cage on all sides and waited for the tournament to begin. Would these prisoners beat death? Everyone knew they wouldn't. No one ever did.

"Time to hide, partner," said the cruel prisoner as he jolted for a tree inside the cage.

But before he had gone far, the earth began to shake and a beastly hand came up through the ground. Flames burst around the beast as it pulled itself up to its feet. As it stood up, it was comparable to the size of a two-story house. "Behemoth," they called him. He had the face of a hippo and the tusks of an elephant. His yellow, reptilian eyes widened with the sight of his prey. The earth shook with every step he took towards the cruel prisoner.

This frightened the kind prisoner and he ran towards a sizable lake inside the cage. It was close enough to the bars that he wondered if perhaps there was a way to swim underneath the cage and out to freedom. But Sarx remained still. He shielded his eyes from the horror as a tear rolled down his cheek. He had no desire to see the death of the prisoners—even the cruel one. The crowd roared as the prisoner's body was crushed by the beast's giant foot. The creature then picked up his corpse and consumed it.

"Sarx!" screamed a familiar voice from behind him. He turned to see the arms of his mother reaching through the bars to embrace him. Standing next to her were Junia, Marie, and Jimmy and Johnny. "My baby!" she yelled in terror as her voice cracked.

"Mama!" he cried as he jammed his face up against the metal poles. She put her arms around him, completely unconcerned about the blood that stained her sleeves. Her face contorted as she placed her hands on his cheeks and moved his hair out of his eyes.

"Please tell me there's another way," she wept as tears soaked her shirt.

# EXECUTION

"I do only what I see my Father is doing. I'm afraid this is my cup to drink," cried Sarx.

"Why?" she bawled. "There has to be another way!"

"Mama. Look at me. This is the only way. I know this is hard to watch, but I need you to be strong for me." He then turned to Johnny. "You will take care of her in my absence, yes?"

A tear fell down Johnny's face. "Yes, Sarx. Whatever you desire."

"And Mama, you will take care of Johnny?"

"Of course, Sarx," she cried. "But I don't want you to go. Not this way. Any way but this way. *Please.*"

Sarx tried to force a smile as tears swelled in his eyes. "I love you Mama," he said.

The crowd erupted in cheers as the head of a huge serpent came swiftly out of the lake and devoured the kind prisoner.

"Hi Sssssarx," Levi hissed as he slowly submerged himself back into the water.

Sarx then let go of his mother, took a deep breath, and began to limp slowly towards the middle of the cage.

"Sarx?" called his mother. "SARX!" she screamed louder. She continued to yell until she could no more, her throat too broken from the pain. She fell into Junia's lap and the two of them bawled together.

Sarx's heart broke more than it had ever been broken as the spiritual weight in the atmosphere grew to unimaginable levels. "God," he prayed quietly as he limped. "Why have you left me here alone?"

The audience grew quiet as a hot wind blew by their faces. But it wasn't exactly like wind. It almost had the pattern of waves, each in sync with a low-pitched whooshing noise that was growing louder and louder.

"It's the Plaintiff!" yelled a child.

The audience was instantly filled with awe and fear. Usually the Plaintiff sent others to do his dirty work—he didn't typically do it himself. But there he was, as beautiful and as terrifying as ever. The great dragon landed on the cage and ripped the bars apart with his metallic claws. The audience cheered as he slithered into the cage.

"Oh, I am going to love thisssss," he hissed as the people laughed.

Sarx stood completely still and didn't say a word.

Smoke came out of the dragon's nostrils as he breathed. "Oh come on now King Sarx—*Son of God, Son of Man*. Surely you're not too ssssshy to talk to your kingdom. Now's a good time to share your last wordsssss."

Still, Sarx did nothing.

"Very well then," growled the Plaintiff. "I guess I'll just have to make you speak!"

The dragon then nailed Sarx down to the floor, holding him under his metallic foot. Sarx could still breathe, though quite uncomfortably.

"Sssspeak," the dragon hissed.

# EXECUTION

Sarx remained quiet.

Two metallic claws extended out of the Plaintiff's foot and were plunged into Sarx's hands.

"Sssssspeak!" he hissed louder.

Sarx let out a yelp of pain, but still said nothing. And so the dragon drove two more metallic claws into his feet.

"SSSSPEAK!" the Plaintiff roared as Sarx cried out and stained the earth with blood. But still he refused to talk. Maria's cry could be heard for miles.

The dragon huffed as black smoke exited his mouth. "Fine. If you are out of words to say, then I will ensure that your final noises are nothing more than cries of pain!"

The dragon then bit into Sarx's heel and used his teeth to toss him high into the air to catch him in his mouth and devour him. The priests watched with excitement.

"There he goes men," said the lead priest. "He certainly was high and lifted up for all to see, wasn't he?" The others laughed.

Sarx's body flew through the air, a bloodied mess. And as he came down, he stretched his arms out wide and whispered, "It is done."

And all went black.

# CHAPTER 27
## Chains

As Sarx came to in the spirit, he noticed many former angels in front of him, each chained to the wall in this gloomy place.

"Welcome to the afterlife," one of them smiled devilishly.

"Who would have thought," said another. "*Thee* Son of God sentenced to the same place as the sons of God."

"Perhaps you don't have to do anything especially wrong to be sentenced here after all," chimed in another. "You could take up human wives and birth your own creation like we did, or you can try your best to complete God's mission and fail and still end up in this place just the same."

Sarx stood up as they continued to talk. "I still can't believe it worked!" cried another. "I didn't think Daystar would actually pull it off!"

"I know!" laughed another. "I mean, we devised a pretty good plan to use Judah against him, but I thought for sure he would call down a legion of angels to help him or something! You did have the power to do that, didn't you Son of God? Or were you really nothing more than a Son of Man in the end? Because you certainly died like one!"

Sarx surveyed the room of chained-up fallen angels and then surveyed his own wrists and feet. "You do realize that I don't have chains on like all of you, right?" he questioned.

The angels paused. "Well sure, but you've still been abandoned here," one replied. "Maybe you have a little more freedom than the rest of us, but you're still stuck."

"I suppose that would be true under normal circumstances," nodded Sarx. "Certainly none of you have ever escaped this place before. You've been stuck down here for centuries and will remain here until the bitter end for your sins." The angels mumbled and huffed at him. "I guess that's the thing though," said Sarx. "I wouldn't say this qualifies as normal circumstances."

"What are you talking about?" yelled an angel.

"Oh come on guys," said Sarx, rolling his eyes. "You know the omniscience of God better than anyone! *Or at least you should.* Do you really think that in God's foresight, he truly did not account for this moment right now?"

"We beat him," hissed an angel. "All the forces of the underworld banded together and we killed you! It's done! You are now a slave to death just like the rest of humanity!"

"Ah yes, the curse of death," said Sarx. "I'm trying to remember—what were the rules on how that worked again?"

"You already know the story," said another angel. "The Plaintiff convinced humanity to pursue the corruption, and their sin brought death into the world. Therefore, all humanity is subject to sin and dies. Simple as that."

"Well that's just the thing," said Sarx. "I don't recall ever sinning."

"Of course you did," said another. "You were human! All humans sin!"

"But you also called me the son of God," said Sarx.

"Well sure, we can see both identities in you," said an angel. "But that doesn't make you sinless. I mean, we were sons of God and we certainly sinned!"

"Check my name in the book of life and you will see that I did, in fact, live a sinless human life," said Sarx. "Which means you all overstepped your bounds and broke the rules when you killed me. And I believe that means that the keys of death are no longer in your authority to carry."

"No!" shouted an angel. "There's no way you lived a sinless life! Only God himself could do that!"

Suddenly Sarx's entire body began to glow the brightest white anyone had ever seen.

"That's right, Azazel," said Sarx. "*I am* the only one who could do that."

# CHAPTER 28
## THE KEYS

Three days after killing Sarx, the Plaintiff suddenly felt incredibly uncomfortable and got up from his throne. Almost as soon as he had stood up, a beam of light cracked through his stomach and a fist reached through it. The dragon roared and fell on his back in pain as Sarx pulled himself through the reptilian skin.

While the Plaintiff was still on his back, Sarx waved his hand across the air and the dragon's metallic legs fell off and rolled into the lava, where they melted in its heat. The dragon roared as fire filled his veins. Sarx then ripped the keys of death and the underworld off of the dragon's neck as he hissed angrily.

The Plaintiff craned his neck over his stomach and began to blow fire into the opening Sarx had created in attempts to cauterize the wound. He then rolled onto his stomach and snapped at Sarx like a snake, but Sarx leapt over the dragon's mouth and landed on his head with such incredible force, that his footprint was permanently lodged into the Plaintiff's skull.

Sarx then waved his hand again and the Plaintiff's metallic wings flew off into the lava and also melted. The snake shook his head furiously, throwing Sarx off the island and into the deep lava. The Plaintiff breathed heavily, his eyes filled with rage and humiliation at the same time. He had won now—he was sure of it.

But then, suddenly, Sarx's head appeared above the lava as he slowly walked back towards the island—his body being revealed inch by inch. The lava rolled off his skin, revealing no damage. The snake's eyes grew huge.

"Face it," Sarx said. "Had you known what killing me would do—*or that my death was a part of the plan all along*—you would have never touched me."

The snake looked confused and terrified.

"Oh, now you're the one who doesn't talk?" Sarx taunted.

Just then, thunder cracked across the sky and water began to rush down into the volcano like a flood, quickly turning the lava into rock.

"What is happening?" hissed the snake. "It doesn't rain here!"

"This," said Sarx, "is the rise of the Water Kingdom."

And instantly Sarx disappeared.

# CHAPTER 29
## Rain

Mason, Junia, and the rest of the gang sat around a campfire on the beach, cooking fish, when rain began to pour in the middle of a cloudless day. The clash between the rain and the sun were so vibrant that the sky lit up with a beautiful rainbow and the whole beach began to glow like a prism. Everywhere they looked, shimmery shades of red, yellow, green and blue were swirling around.

"It's beautiful, isn't it?" asked a familiar voice.

Everyone turned around immediately to see what they thought was a ghost. Sarx was letting off a soft glow while whittling the end of a long stick. He walked towards Mason.

"Sarx?" Mason asked. "Are you… are you a spirit?"

"No," answered Sarx with a smile. "I told you I would give you evidence that resurrection is real before all of this was over." He then glanced down at Mason's arm. "Let me see it, friend."

Mason blushed, embarrassed to be a disgusting scaly creature in front of such a glorious man. "I'm not worthy, Sarx," he said. "I'm not qualified for this job."

"Let me see your arm," Sarx said again as he reached out and grabbed it.

Mason rolled his eyes in embarrassment. "I've tried everything to get rid of it. I just can't seem to wash it off," he said.

"Of course not," Sarx said. "You've already been washed, but you still need me to take care of the dust that you kick up day by day." Sarx pulled at a scale causing Mason to inhale sharply through his teeth. "That is pretty stuck," said Sarx. "Your shame holds it tightly to your skin."

"Well of course I'm ashamed! I deserve to be ashamed!" cried Mason. "You put so much hope in me and I left you hanging! I denied you to everyone I met and left you to die in a cage! I heard the stories of what they did to you—we all heard the stories! How are you even here right now?"

"I told you," said Sarx. "Resurrection is a different kind of life. It doesn't work the same as life as you know it now."

Mason wiped a few tears from his eyes as Sarx continued to look at his scales.

"Mason," said Sarx. "Do you love me?"

Mason closed his watery eyes tightly. "I know it's hard to believe given the way that I've been acting, but yes, I do. I really, really do."

## THE RISE OF THE WATER KINGDOM

Sarx rubbed his hand across Mason's arm and a third of the scales fell off.

"Then take care of those who join me in expanding the kingdom," he said. "Mason, do you love me?" he asked again.

Mason sniffed. "I just said yes. You know I do."

"Then take care of those who join me in expanding the kingdom," he said as he rubbed another third of the scales off of his arm. He then repeated the question again. "Mason, do you love me?"

"Yes," said Mason. "I… *I know I love you.*" Sarx rubbed his arm one last time as the final scales fell off. "And I will take care of those who join you in expanding your kingdom."

Sarx smiled and began to walk towards a dock on the sea.

"Wait, where are you going?" asked Junia as she wiped the rain from her face.

"I'm a king!" laughed Sarx. "I have a throne in Heaven to attend to!"

"Wait, but then how will you lead your citizens on earth?" Junia yelled to him.

"My Spirit—the Spirit of Light will guide you and all who join you!" he said.

"You mean God's Spirit?" Bart called back.

"That's what I said," winked Sarx. "*My Spirit!*"

And with that, he dived off the dock into the water, but vanished while still in the air.

Bart looked around at his drenched friends as the rain continued to pour.

# RAIN

"Uh, guys," Bart said. "Who exactly did we just spend the last few days with?"

# WRITER'S NOTE
## Allegory

I'm primarily a non-fiction writer. I love to study and wrestle with the Bible and try to bring it to life for others. That being said, when it comes to the little fiction I do read and write, allegory is my favorite—simply because that's exactly what allegory does: It studies and wrestles with the Bible and then tries to bring it to life for others in a new way.

But that being said, I did not intend to be quite as allegorical as this book ended up being. I wasn't aiming for Lord of the Rings where symbolism and metaphor is often very distant, but something more like Narnia, where a story separate from the Bible is told, but the Bible story is incorporated into it in unique ways. That was how this book started: Two siblings in a forest waiting for a Jesus-like-wizard-figure to show up.

But as I wrote, things shifted. The Jesus-like-wizard-figure became incredibly obvious. Soon I felt like I wasn't really writing a separate allegorical story, but

## ALLEGORY

instead I felt as though I was trying to rewrite the gospel story with a fantasy bend.

There were times where this made me quite uncomfortable. Due to the obvious nature of everything, I felt at times like I was interjecting my own studies, thoughts, and beliefs into the mouth of Sarx. Because of that, I feared people might hear what he had to say and take it as though Jesus Himself had said it–especially since so many don't read their Bibles these days.

Don't get me wrong: I tried to get Sarx's voice to speak what I do believe the Word of God teaches, but obviously I am a flawed, errant human being that plenty would disagree with, regardless of whether I am wrong or right. And that's why non-fiction is safer to write; for we often read non-fiction expecting to disagree with the author here and there. But when we get attached to the characters we've created, we read their words differently. This, of course, can carry a world of good–*God knows how deeply touched I am by most of Aslan's words in Narnia*–but again, allegory has its dangers too.

That being said, if you'd like to learn more about how I believe the Bible confirms some of the allegorical interpretations I've communicated throughout this book, see either my short book, *Fantasy IRL: Glimpses of a Hidden World,* or its lengthy companion, *The Rush and the Rest: The Supernatural World and the Holy Spirit.* The latter will especially dive into the Biblical evidence behind many of my views.

I pray that the Holy Spirit has worked alongside this book in someway to open you up to the gospel and the fuller story the Bible paints from beginning to end. But that being said, He will work alongside no book better than His own, so I encourage you to study His written word for true insight.

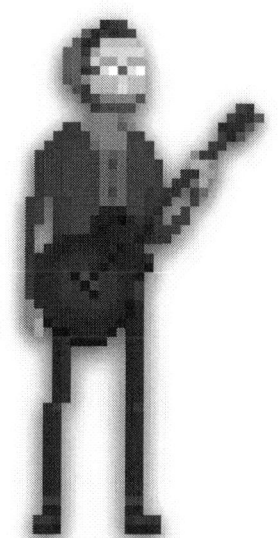

# ABOUT THE AUTHOR

Jamin is ordained in the Free Methodist Church and is the lead pastor of 1208GREENWOOD in downtown Jackson, MI. He and his wife Jodi have two energetic kids named Beckett and Jericho who love to keep them on their toes. Outside of pastoring and writing, Jamin loves video games, board games, grilling, entertaining guests, and writing, recording and playing music. His other books and audiobooks include, *A Taste of Jesus, Alien Theology, The Rush and the Rest, Kaiju of Biblical Proportions, Fantasy IRL*, and even a stick figure comic book called, *Calligraphy Sticks*.

Made in the USA
Middletown, DE
27 August 2019